*Danger
at
Niagara*

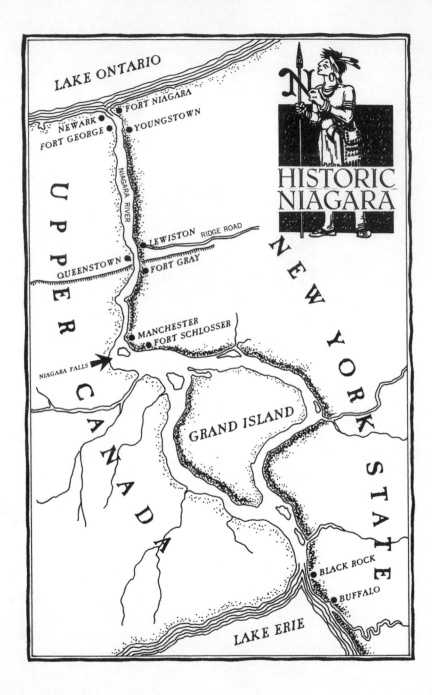

LAKE ONTARIO

FORT NIAGARA

NEWARK
FORT GEORGE

YOUNGSTOWN

U P P E R

NIAGARA RIVER

HISTORIC
NIAGARA

N E W

LEWISTON   RIDGE ROAD

QUEENSTOWN   FORT GRAY

Y O R K

MANCHESTER
FORT SCHLOSSER

NIAGARA FALLS

C A N A D A

GRAND ISLAND

S T A T E

BLACK ROCK

BUFFALO

LAKE ERIE

Danger at Niagara

BY *Margaret Goff Clark*

ILLUSTRATED BY ERNEST KURT BARTH

FUNK & WAGNALLS   *New York*

To Marcia—my Molly

Author's Note

Since some of the place names used in this book have changed since the time of my story, the reader might like to know the following:

Fort Schlosser—was the site of an old fort at the southern end of the portage around the falls of Niagara. It is now part of the city of Niagara Falls, New York.

Lewiston—was originally called Lewis Town in honor of Governor Lewis of New York State.

Manchester—is now called Niagara Falls, New York.

Newark—is now called Niagara-on-the-Lake.

Queenstown—is a Canadian village that was originally named Queens Town for Queen Charlotte of England. The name gradually has shortened to the present Queenston.

In this Note, I should like also to thank the following people for assistance in gathering and checking historical information used in my book:

Donald E. Loker, Executive Director, Old Fort Niagara

Dr. Louis L. Tucker, State Historian of New York

Clarence O. Lewis, Niagara County Historian

Marjorie F. Williams, Niagara Falls City Historian

Jeannette Wylie, Supervisor of Social Studies, Niagara Falls
Public Schools

Helen Kimball, formerly Town of Lewiston Historian

Ruth E. Witmer, Local History Librarian, Niagara Falls
Public Library

Jane Van Arsdale, Curator of Rare Books, Buffalo and Erie
County Public Library

Alice Pickup, Reference Librarian, Buffalo and Erie County
Historical Society Library

Richard Cary, Jr., Lewiston Town and Village Historian

Grove McClellan, Executive Vice President (Retired), Old
Fort Niagara Association

And, for instruction in musketry, I am indebted to Hubert
E. Torrence, Program Coordinator at Old Fort Niagara.

🔫 M. G. C.

Contents

Chapter 1. Night Raid 🔫 9

Chapter 2. Mischief in Homespun 🔫 16

Chapter 3. The Road to Fort Niagara 🔫 22

Chapter 4. Homan Makes an Enemy 🔫 31

Chapter 5. Village in Flames 🔫 40

Chapter 6. Is Guy a Tory? 🔫 48

Chapter 7. Arrival at Night 🔫 56

Chapter 8. Zeb Takes the Canoe 🔫 65

Chapter 9. Homan Is Needed 🔫 72

Chapter 10. A Dangerous Game 🔫 79

Chapter 11. Flight from Death 🔫 88

Chapter 12. Hardscrabble Camp 🔫 99

Chapter 13. In Enemy Territory 🔫 107

Chapter 14. A Spy Is Unmasked 🔫 117

Chapter 15. Peace 🔫 125

Chapter 1

Night Raid

Exhausted from a day of fruitless hunting, Homan Reed ate a cold supper of cornbread and milk. Hastily he banked the fire and then fell into bed, forgetting his loneliness and the ever-present danger from across the river.

He awoke at dawn, shivering under the heavy quilts, awakened as much by the silence as the cold. He lay still, listening. Gray morning light came through the small panes of glass Uncle Oliver had carried all the way from Connecticut. A sound that usually penetrated the log walls of the cabin was missing—a sound that was part of the background of his life in this lonely frontier clearing in western New York State.

His heart began to beat too fast, and he sat up in bed, reaching for the buckskin breeches he had laid on top of the quilts. Homan was a good-looking boy, rather small for his almost fifteen years. He pulled on heavy woolen socks and then thrust his feet into sturdy shoepacks with firm leather soles and flexible deerskin tops that fastened well above his ankles. They were still damp and stiff from yesterday's long pursuit of an elusive deer. But Homan was unaware of how cold they were, for alarm was making his blood race. He snatched up his warm coat and let himself out of the door. It was about eight in the morning, but with the overcast sky it seemed more like early evening. Even so, he could easily see the tracks in the snow— fresh tracks of moccasins and boots, and deep hoof marks. With a strangled cry, he raced to the rear of the cabin, then across the trampled snow to the barn. The door stood open— and the barn was empty! Belinda, the cow, and the twenty plump chickens were gone. It was the lowing of the cow he had missed, and the morning shout of the rooster.

Frantically, Homan looked about the dim barn, hoping to see Belinda hiding in a shadowy corner. There was no movement and no sound.

Pulling his coat more tightly around his body, he began to follow the trail in the snow. It led to the west, toward the river a hundred yards away, heading, as he had guessed it would, for the gully that split the river bank. The tracks of cow and men went down the sloping path where in summer he had taken Belinda to the river for a drink. They continued to the water's edge and there they stopped. His sharp eyes noted a small round object in one of the footprints at the top of the bank. He snatched it up and examined it. A button—a British regimental button!

Homan stared bitterly across the swift gray Niagara River to the Canadian shore. The cow Uncle Oliver had worked so hard to buy, the chickens that had given them cherished eggs —all were gone. Why even now British soldiers were probably milking Belinda while their cooks wrung the necks of some of the chickens. Milk and chicken dinner for the enemy, but only hunger for him and the neighbors he had supplied with milk and eggs.

He was furious with himself for sleeping so soundly. Why hadn't he heard the raiding party that had stolen across in the night and led Belinda to the river? Why hadn't he heard her bawling? Surely she wouldn't go peaceably with strangers, especially since some of them must have been the Mohawks who were allied with the British, and she would be afraid of the smell of the bear grease they smeared on their skin. He must have been tired, indeed, to have slept through the noise of the chickens squawking and the sound of the soldiers' boots crunching on the snow.

This was the last straw! He had had all he could stand of being on the sidelines. He guessed he was a War Hawk like Henry Clay and John Calhoun and Peter Porter. Long before the war started, those men had spoken in Congress and declared that the United States had to stand up for her rights and not let the British kidnap seamen off American ships. Homan's brother, Guy, and their uncle, Oliver Reed, had not agreed with the War Hawks. Homan remembered how the three of them had sat before their fire arguing about the first rumblings of a war that then seemed as far from their little farm on the Niagara River as the Pole Star.

"There's no need to go to war," Uncle Oliver had said. "The British government and ours could solve these problems in a day's conference."

Homan had protested, "The British act as if they still own us. We can't put up with that."

"It isn't that simple," said Guy. "We have some land-hungry politicians who believe we can take Canada if we go to war."

Homan said with confidence, "Most Canadians would be happy to be part of the United States."

"Would *you* like to be taken over by Canada?" demanded Guy.

"Of course not!" Homan cried. "We're a free country! But Canada isn't."

Uncle Oliver had leaned forward to stir the fire. "Peace, Homan," he had said in his gentle way. "If you had fought in the War of Independence as I did, you'd never want to see another war."

Homan had stopped then because he could see his uncle was deeply upset, and he wanted never to hurt the man who had given a home to him and Guy when their parents had died three years before.

But the war had come, just the same. It had been going on for more than a year now, ever since June of 1812. Uncle Oliver, though he had wanted nothing to do with the war, was dead because of it. And Guy, who was as peace-loving as Uncle Oliver, had enlisted as soon as he was eighteen. Homan wondered what Guy would say when he knew that the cow and chickens had been stolen.

The river below him was deep and full of treacherous currents, and now in December, it was icy cold, of course. It was possible the cow had not lived to reach the opposite shore.

Halfway down the river bank, to the right of the gully, Homan and his Indian friend, David Cusick, had hidden their canoe. Homan wished he dared paddle across the river to look for Belinda, but he knew it would mean capture or death for him to land on the Canadian shore at this point. Farther downstream near Fort George he might have a chance, for the Americans had held that fort for the past six months. In fact, Guy was stationed there now.

Impulsively, Homan scrambled down the bank to make absolutely sure the canoe had not been discovered by the enemy. He and Dave had made it themselves, and it was a prized possession. There it was, in plain sight, twenty feet or so to the right of the gully. That was strange. The last time he had looked at it, it had been well hidden under branches and snow. He clambered across the steep bank. There was no doubt about it, the canoe had been moved. He examined the ground nearby. Not even the fresh snow could completely hide the deep footprints that led to the edge of the water.

With his mouth set in a grim line, Homan carried the canoe farther up the bank, where he laid it across two logs under the drooping branches of a willow tree. It was possible that Dave had used the canoe, but Homan doubted it. Dave would have made sure it was hidden from view. Still, if the British had used it, why had they brought it back?

Suddenly he realized that he had come out without his cap or mittens. The biting wind was raking through his shaggy brown hair, and his fingers were numb. He climbed the bank and left the river with determination growing in him. No matter who was to blame for this war and no matter what had caused it, it had to be fought and won before he and other settlers like him could work in peace and safety.

He had been determined to join the army when his brother had volunteered six months before, but Guy had said flatly, "You're too young."

"Matt Pomeroy is signing up," Homan retorted. Matt was his best friend. "He isn't much older than I am."

"He's seventeen, as you well know," replied Guy, "and he's footloose. With us, it's different. We have the farm and Belinda. We don't want to sell her. You know how hard it is to get a good milch cow, and after the war we'll need her."

"Let the Warrens keep her," Homan suggested. "They need the milk." The Warrens were their nearest neighbors and good friends.

"Sure, they need the milk," Guy agreed, "but they don't have room in the shed for their oxen and Belinda and the feed. Besides, Anne and Molly have all the work they can handle now. No, you move in with the Warrens and go back and forth to milk the cow and collect the eggs."

"I have a better idea," Homan announced. "*You* stay home and I'll enlist!"

"Don't be silly," Guy said wearily. "How could I let my little brother go in my place?"

Homan flushed. "Your *little* brother is tall enough to carry a gun," he said.

"Don't get excited. I wasn't referring to your size. Look, I *have* to join up." Guy's voice shook with emotion. "I'm not sure I want to, but I can't respect myself if I don't. And someone has to take care of Belinda and the farm. Now, don't make it harder for me. I'll speak to Rufus Warren about letting you board there."

Homan answered stubbornly, "If I have to stay out of the army to take care of a cow and chickens, I'll live right in our own cabin."

Well, now that Belinda and the chickens were gone there was nothing to keep him here. In another month he would be fifteen. Surely that was old enough for a soldier, and Guy, across the river at Fort George, couldn't stop him. By the time he reached the cabin, he had made up his mind. He was going to Fort Niagara and enlist this very day.

Inside the one-room cabin, he broke off a piece of johnny-cake and drained the remaining jug of milk that was in the larder. Then he quickly stuffed some extra socks and undergarments into a knapsack. There was no need to pack a shirt or pants. He'd get a uniform from the army—a blue uniform, probably. He had heard, though, that the government had run out of blue cloth and had had to make some trousers and jackets of gray- or drab-colored cloth.

He put on his warm cap of fox fur, thrust his hands into his mittens, and started for the door. There he checked himself and returned for the musket that hung over the fireplace. Uncle Oliver had carried it in the War for Independence and Homan used it for hunting. Carefully, he went over it, making sure it was well oiled and ready. Probably the army would supply him with a gun, but he was accustomed to this one and he felt he could depend on it. He would also take along a few of the cartridges he had made up of powder and shot wrapped in a twist of paper. With them he could load his musket more quickly. Then, swinging his powder horn and leather shot pouch over his shoulder, he again went to the rough plank door.

As he lifted the latch, something hit the outside of the door with a solid thud. The enemy had returned! But what else did they want? Were they after *him* this time?

Chapter 2

Mischief in Homespun

Homan dropped the latch and thrust home the bar Uncle Oliver had put on the door for use in time of danger. He had heard no shot, so it must have been an arrow that struck the door. That meant Indians. Of course, the Mohawks had guns, but sometimes they still used arrows, and their aim was deadly accurate.

He crept to the window and peered out, but he could see no one. Then a faint sound caught his ear, a sound suspiciously like a giggle, and into his line of vision came a girl of about fourteen. She wore a bonnet tied under her chin and a long brown homespun skirt that dragged in the snow. Her mischievous eyes laughed up into his through the window. It was Molly Warren!

Instead of an Indian attack, it was Molly up to her usual

tricks. He should have known. He flung open the door and, to his embarrassment, saw on it the round, unmistakable mark of a snowball.

He glared at Molly. "You're lucky I didn't shoot you!"

"Some soldier you'd be!" Molly taunted him. "Scared of a snowball."

"How'd I know it was a snowball?" demanded Homan. "You ought to know better—what with a war going on."

Molly's brown eyes still danced. "I thought you'd realize it was my kind of trick, really I did."

Homan did not relent. Her father might give in at a glance from those pretty eyes, but *he* wouldn't. "If you think this war's such a joke, look there." He gestured toward the barn.

Molly glanced at the open barn door, then down at the heavily trodden snow, and ran toward the barn. She was a little taller than Homan and slim as a heron. Homan watched her run, pleased to see her, even though he wouldn't admit it even to himself. She was a nuisance, a pest, and it was time she learned life wasn't just a game.

He followed her to the barn, and when she turned around, her face had lost its merriment. "Mohawks?" she asked.

"And soldiers," he said. "I found a button from a British uniform and there are boot marks. See?"

She gazed at the trampled snow and shuddered. "So close to the cabin. They might have killed you." She looked up at him. "I wonder they didn't."

Why, Molly cared what happened to him! "Maybe they got all they wanted—this time," he answered.

Molly's eyes seemed even darker than usual as she walked back to the cabin with him. "You can't live here now. Come and stay with us. There's a bed in the loft."

"No." Homan was eager to be on his way to the fort.

"There's no reason for me to stay around here now. I'm joining up."

"Guy doesn't want you to enlist. I heard him tell Anne. He said you were too young, and——"

"Too small?" Homan drew in his breath sharply. "I have to do what I think is right."

Molly studied him in silence, and Homan thought he read approval in her dark eyes.

A blast of wind rushed across the clearing and flung a spray of snow against the back of Molly's bonnet and into Homan's face. "Come inside," he said abruptly. "It isn't much warmer, but at least it's out of the wind. Say, what brings you here, anyway?"

"Jeremy's sick." As she mentioned her little brother's name, a new tenderness came into her voice.

Homan, too, had a special fondness for four-year-old Jeremy. Whenever he visited the Warrens, the little fellow was at his heels like a puppy. Homan liked taking him small gifts—a dog he carved from a piece of wood, a handful of chestnuts or beechnuts, the first bright autumn leaves.

Molly went on, "Yesterday he was feverish and last night he kept crying out. Anne and I were up with him a dozen times. I thought maybe an egg might taste good to him, and we used the last of ours yesterday." As if struck for the first time with the enormity of the loss, she exclaimed, "What will we do without Belinda's milk? And the eggs? You and Guy have been so kind about bringing them to us."

It made Homan uncomfortable to hear her thanks for the milk and eggs. Often enough he had grumbled when Guy had told him to carry the pail of milk and the basket of eggs the mile through the forest to the Warren home in Lewiston. He should have been glad to do anything he could for the Warrens. It was Molly's father, Rufus, who had pulled Uncle Oliver out of the cold river that October day when a sniper from the Canadian shore had shot him. Oliver Reed had died, but at least he had died in his own bed, with his two nephews beside him.

Homan picked up a basket that contained six eggs. "You can have these. They're all that's left." He opened the door. "Come on. I'll see you home and then come back for my things."

With head bent against the wind, he led the way across the clearing to the well-worn path that the Reeds and the Warrens had beaten through the woods. It was warmer in the shelter of the great trees, but only a gloomy light filtered through the brown leaves that still clung to the oaks. Homan could hear them rustling in the wind high above, like a crowd of people whispering.

"You shouldn't have come here alone," he scolded Molly. "Some Mohawk might still be hiding around here."

"By daylight?" Molly scoffed. "Anne didn't see me go," she added with a grin. "I wanted to do *something* to make Jeremy feel better. What *can* we do?"

Homan shook his head sympathetically. Fevers were terrible things. When a fever struck, even the doctors were helpless. His own father and mother had died from typhus, and last winter hundreds on the Niagara Frontier—among them Molly's mother—had been buried as a result of typhoid or "Smyth Fever," as the settlers called it, naming it for the unpopular General Alexander Smyth.

When they came within sight of the Warren cabin, Homan stopped. "I'll go back now. Will you tell Major Bennett about Belinda and the chickens?" The report ought to be made to the commander of the militia at Lewiston even though Homan doubted that it would do any good. Most of the militia had gone home, saying Fort Niagara and Fort Gray would protect Lewiston. Even if they were here in force, they wouldn't send an expedition into Canada to rescue a cow. Anyway, Homan had little faith in the poorly trained state militia. Look at the way they had acted when Van Rensselaer tried to take Queenstown Heights, across the river from Lewiston. A few of them had gone over in the first boats with the regular army men. But then the rest of them had remained on the river bank at Lewiston while their comrades died for want of reinforcements. "We're New York State militia," they had said. "We don't have to leave the boundary of our own state."

Homan had viewed the battle with Uncle Oliver and Guy that autumn day over a year ago, and although he thought the militia should cross, he could see why they were reluctant to go. Not only was the musket and cannon fire heavy on the other side, but there were few pilots who knew the treacherous Niagara River currents. Lothrop Cooke, who had run a ferry across to Canada before the war, was one of the best pilots and he had gone back and forth across the river all day, until he had injured his leg and had to be carried home.

Uncle Oliver's face had turned gray as he watched and his eyes had taken on a hard, bright shine. Suddenly he said, "I can row a boat and I know something about these currents. I'm going to take Lothrop's place." With that he had gone down to the ferry landing and volunteered to man a boat. And only a little while later, he had been fatally wounded.

Homan now became aware that Molly was staring at him.

"What are you thinking about when you get that funny look on your face?" she asked.

"Just woolgathering." Homan gave Molly a playful shove toward the cabin.

She looked back at him over her shoulder. "Come in for a bite of hot breakfast. There's porridge left."

Homan was tempted, but he was restless, eager to be on his way. With a wave of his hand, he returned to the forest trail. Almost at once he regretted his decision. He *was* hungry and the trail ahead was lonely. The warm cabin and the friendly people drew him, but he would not turn back. He squared his shoulders. He'd accept no charity. Many times he had eaten at the Warrens' table, but he had gone fortified by the knowledge that the milk and eggs he supplied to them at a modest price were helping to pay for what he ate.

Molly had said he could stay there, but they really didn't need him. Rufus Warren was a strong and capable man, and since he was stationed at Fort Gray, near Lewiston, he could get home every day or so. Molly and seventeen-year-old Anne ran the house as well as grown women could have done.

Homan was convinced his place was with the army, fighting to protect Molly and Anne—and Jeremy. He wished now he had gone in for just a look at Jeremy. If the little fellow didn't get well——. Firmly, Homan shut this idea out of his mind.

Chapter 3

The Road to Fort Niagara

Snow began to fall before Homan reached his cabin. He saw one flake and then another drop between the branches and drift to the ground like feathers from a gull. By the time he reached the clearing, fresh drifts were already leaning against the fence and the wind-whipped snow made it difficult to see the cabin.

He stopped only long enough to pick up his things and to tuck a package of johnnycake inside the front of his shirt. Then he set out again. This time he took the River Road and headed north toward Fort Niagara. It was a stormy day, but now that his decision was made, he was impatient to get to the fort.

The river was on his left. Sometimes the road edged the bank and at other times it moved inland several hundred feet, leaving a wall of trees between it and the swift water. Here the Niagara River looked like a chained tiger, Homan thought, but behind him, seven miles south of Lewiston, where it plunged roaring over the cliff, it was wild and free.

The musket weighed heavily on his arm, but he was accustomed to carrying it on long hunting excursions. Ever since he had moved from Connecticut to Uncle Oliver's cabin on the Niagara River three years before, he and his Tuscarora friend, Dave Cusick, had often roamed the countryside together. Sometimes if night fell when they were far from home, they made beds of boughs and took turns feeding a fire to keep away wild animals.

Busy with his thoughts, he strode along only half-conscious of the snow that was piling up in the narrow road. He wondered how Guy liked being a soldier. Not much, he guessed, because Guy was no fighter. He always tried to settle an argument without blows. For a long while it had looked as if he weren't going to sign up at all. He had always listened to their uncle, and the last thing Oliver Reed had said before he died, was, "Guy, don't you be foolish. You stay out of this war."

Homan knew his brother had done a lot of thinking before he enlisted. Whenever letters came from their cousins back in Connecticut, he read them over and over until they were worn with handling. The cousins had no use for the war and they wrote that all of New England was about ready to break off from the rest of the States over it.

"We need more years of peace," they wrote, "so we can build up our trade with the rest of the world."

Guy had nodded his agreement as he read. But then one night when he and Homan had been at the Warrens' for supper, the talk as usual had turned to the war.

"Can't say I blame the militia for refusing to cross the river to Queenstown," Rufus said. He fished a glowing branch from the fire to light his pipe. "They could see 'twas tantamount to suicide with that battery over at Vrooman's Point killing men as fast as they came across. Besides, it takes training to make a soldier. If they were trained like the British army, for instance, our militia would be the best fighting men in the world, because they have a country they're proud to fight for."

Anne, who was clearing the plates from the table, had paused with both hands full. She made a pretty picture with her light brown hair lying soft on her shoulders and the firelight making her eyes shine like a sapphire Homan had once seen on a lady's finger.

"If I were a man, I'd have gone across," she said. Her face flushed as she spoke, for everyone turned to look at her with surprise. She rarely had anything to say when the men were talking.

Her father laughed. "Well, listen to our little War Hawk. I had no idea you felt that way."

"I don't like fighting," she agreed. "But—maybe we have to," she finished lamely.

No more was said, but Homan had seen his brother's face. It had turned a deeper red than Anne's. Two weeks later, Guy had announced that he was joining up.

Through the whirl of flakes ahead of him, Homan saw a dark figure step into the road from the right. He stopped, prepared to leap behind the nearest tree, but a familiar voice called out, "Greeting, Homan!"

Homan laughed and ran forward. "Dave Cusick!"

The tall young Indian smiled delightedly and shifted the cloth bag he was carrying so he could shake hands the way white men did when they met. He was dressed much the same as Homan, except that instead of a coat, he had a blanket draped about him and he was wearing snowshoes of his own making.

"What are you doing?" Homan asked. He stepped off the road into the shelter of the woods and leaned his musket against the trunk of a beechnut tree.

"Checking traps." Dave held up a bag. "One ringtail." He joined Homan in the comparative shelter of the trees and opened the sack so his friend could see the stiff form of the raccoon inside. "You hunt in snow?" he asked. "You have magic gun?"

Homan chuckled. "No, I'm not hunting. I'm going to Fort Niagara." He removed his cap and shook off the snow. "Something happened this morning, something bad." He told Dave about the theft of Belinda and the chickens.

"You go fight now?"

"Yes."

Dave gestured toward Canada. "You go because they take your cow?"

"Well, partly because of that. I wanted to join before, but Guy convinced me it was my duty to take care of the cow and chickens."

Dave's dark brown eyes were fastened steadily on Homan. "Maybe they not take you. My father go to fort with many, many Tuscarora braves when war start. He want to help white friends. At fort they tell him, 'Go home. This not your war.'" Dave lifted his head proudly. "My father good American. He was scout for General Lafayette in other war with British."

"I know," said Homan. "And our generals have found out they need the Indians. They need all the help they can get. That's why I'm volunteering."

"I go part way to fort with you." Dave wrapped his blanket more closely about his shoulders and set off down the road at an easy, rhythmic gait.

Glad of his friend's company, Homan hurried after him, wishing he, too, had worn snowshoes. At best, he could not keep up with Dave's long legs, and today the drifting snow was an added obstacle. Noticing this, Dave slowed down.

They had traveled for half a mile when the Indian seized Homan's arm and pulled him off the road. "Man come," he said softly.

Seconds later a man appeared, stalking down the road with a musket over his shoulder. When he reached the boys' tracks in the snow, he hastily primed his gun, and shouted, "Halt, or I'll fire!"

Homan leaped into the road. "We're friends!" he cried.

The man leveled his gun at Homan, who fell back a few paces. The musket might not discharge in this dampness, but the bayonet that gleamed at the end of its barrel would surely work.

Homan recognized Alex Millar, a boy about his own age who lived near Lewiston.

"Don't you recognize me, Alex?" he asked. "I'm on the way to Fort Niagara to enlist."

"Oh, Homan." The sentry looked relieved. "I swear I expect every shadow to be an Indian."

Dave said solemnly, pointing to himself, "Indian here."

Alex leaned closer. "Aren't you one of Chief Nicholas Cusick's boys?"

Dave nodded, still unsmiling, though Homan glimpsed a twinkle in his eyes.

"You're a good Indian," said the young soldier. "You Tuscaroras are on our side. It's the Mohawks I don't want to see."

"Mohawk good Indians," Dave said. "They have other white friends."

To Homan this was a new idea, but it probably was true that the English and Canadians had the same friendly ties with the Mohawks that the Americans had with the Tuscaroras.

"Are you on duty alone?" Homan asked Alex.

"Yes. The other sentry left an hour ago. He said there was no use patrolling along here in this storm."

Dave spoke up. "Good time for enemy. Snow hide his boats."

Alex said, "That's just what I thought, too." He shouldered his gun. "Say, if you're headed for the fort, you'll want the password." He leaned close to Homan and cupping one hand beside his mouth, said quietly, "Remember the Chesapeake."

Homan repeated the password and added, "I thank you."

Alex saluted, and with a sigh marched off to the south.

"He's the first sentry I've seen today," Homan remarked. "They're supposed to be posted every few rods along the river."

"They get cold," said Dave. "They go in tepee."

"Jolly protection they are."

"Maybe this not their war."

Homan glanced sharply at Dave, but his face was impassive. Sometimes it was impossible to tell when an Indian was serious and when he was joking. He remembered the canoe. Perhaps Dave had moved it for a joke.

"Did you use our canoe?" he asked.

Dave shook his head. "Last time I ride in canoe I go with you. We catch fish."

"Then someone else used it," said Homan. "It was moved."

The snow began to lessen and by the time they reached the Five Mile Meadows, the air was so clear they could see the wide, flat meadow that extended from the foot of the rise where they were standing to the edge of the water.

Homan pulled out his johnnycake and with numb fingers broke off a piece for Dave.

The Indian nodded his thanks and set his game bag on the ground. "This good landing place," he remarked. His quick, dark eyes took in the deserted meadow and shoreline. "Guard belong here."

Homan shivered and told himself it was because of the cold. He saw all too clearly how the British and their Indians, the Mohawks, could land on this undefended meadow and surprise the settlers up and down the river, just as last night they had crept up the gully and stolen his cow and chickens.

"There's supposed to be a guard here," he said. "Maybe he's down by the river."

Dave shrugged. He finished the last of his johnnycake and picked up the bag containing the dead raccoon. "I go now," he said, and turned east into the woods that extended back from the river for miles.

For a moment Homan stared at the oblong marks his friend's snowshoes had left on the fresh snow. Then he continued on the road to the north. Now that he was alone, he felt the cold more keenly. It seemed an eternity before he saw ahead of him the little village of Youngstown. He passed the Swain house and a blacksmith shop set in the hollow where the English had ambushed the French in the Battle of La Belle Famille. That had been in 1759, over fifty years ago. Ever since then the stream that ran along here had been called Bloody Run.

Today the main street of Youngstown was almost deserted. Two horses were tied to the hitching rail outside Campbell's Tavern, and a woman hurried down the street clutching a shawl that looked inadequate for this weather. For the most part people were staying indoors, partially, Homan guessed, because of the cold and partially because it was time for the midday meal.

When he reached Young's Store, he ducked inside to warm himself by the fire. A rich, sharp scent arose from a huge wheel of cheese that sat on the counter opposite the fireplace. He resisted temptation as long as he could, and then he rummaged in his shot pouch until he found a coin to buy a small wedge for himself. This he ate with the scraps of johnnycake that remained, and found it a tasty meal.

He was thirsty, but he had no money for milk or cider. When he went outside, he scooped up a handful of fresh snow and let it dissolve in his mouth.

"Come over here!" A soldier crouched behind a battery on the nearby river bank called out. He had a tiny fire going and over it hung a pot containing a dark liquid. He dipped a cup into the pot and offered it to Homan, saying, "This is better than snow."

The liquid proved to be strong tea, so hot that Homan could feel its warmth all the way down to his stomach. He squatted beside the fire to finish drinking it.

The soldier motioned to the strong earthworks at their backs. "That's one good use for salt, eh?"

Homan looked at him inquiringly.

"You must've heard," said the man. He patted the snow-covered earth behind him. "This is the one and only Salt Battery. Barrels and barrels of salt are buried under here."

"I remember hearing something about it," Homan replied. "A ship came here about the time the war started. A ship loaded with salt. Isn't that right?"

"Two ships," the soldier corrected him. "And it was just after we got word we were at war. You never saw any sailors unload ships so fast. They didn't want those guns over at Fort George blowing them to pieces. Someone in Youngstown got the idea of making a battery here, so they piled up the barrels of salt and covered them with dirt. Now that our troops are holding Fort George, this battery's a quiet spot. But we keep the cannons ready." He nodded toward the two twelve-pound cannons that nosed over the earthworks. "I hear the British are crowding in on Fort George. These big guns may be needed sooner than we think."

Chapter 4

Homan Makes an Enemy

Only a mile lay between the Salt Battery and Fort Niagara, but a bitter north wind was now blowing and Homan had to walk directly into it. He pulled up his scarf to cover his nose and ears. Every now and then he walked backward to ease the sting of the wind. He thought his face and hands might freeze before he reached the fort.

As he struggled forward, he heard a whining noise in the woods on his right. He paused to listen. It sounded like an animal, an animal in pain. Homan waded through a waist-high drift at the edge of the road and advanced several paces into the woodland, where he paused again to listen. This time the cry was nearer, and following the sound, he located a small black dog cowering in the snow.

Homan propped his gun against a tree and knelt beside the

animal. "Now, little fellow," he said, "you're going to be all right." As he had guessed, the dog's right front foot was caught in a trap, but in a moment, he had it free. The dog ran a few limping steps and then looked expectantly at him.

"Let's see your foot," Homan said. The trap was a small one, so he was quite sure the dog was not seriously hurt.

Homan held out his hand, and after a moment's hesitation the dog came up to him. The foot had been cut by the trap, Homan discovered, but the bone was not broken. It should heal and be as good as new before long.

"Go home," he ordered. But when he returned to the road, the dog followed him. Homan pointed sternly to the south, but as soon as he moved on, the dog went with him.

As Homan approached Fort Niagara, he felt a bit frightened. Several times during the past three years he had visited the fort, but this was the first time he had come alone. Well, practically alone. He looked down at the little dog and wondered if animals were welcome behind those forbidding walls. This one certainly seemed to have adopted him. Homan wondered about the dog's ancestry. He looked like a retriever—a small retriever, the runt of the litter. His short black hair was glossy and his nose thrust forward inquisitively, but his eyes were his most appealing feature. Alert, friendly, and unafraid, they were fastened hopefully on Homan.

"I'll have no place to keep you," Homan said to the dog. But the animal seemed to take the pleasant voice as a good sign and wagged his tail as he led the way toward the fort.

The earthworks and wooden ramparts appeared even more imposing than usual with their topping of snow. To keep up his courage, Homan reminded himself that his friend Matt Pomeroy was inside the fort.

His steps slowed. Just beyond him the road forked. The left

branch sloped down to the docks and buildings of Trader Town where several stores and warehouses huddled on a flat piece of land below the ramparts of the fort. Straight ahead was the main gateway to the fort. Before he could find Matt he would have to cross the drawbridge under the very nose of the cannons that guarded the entrance.

As he lingered at the edge of the woods, Homan saw a small man in a blue army uniform run up the road from Trader Town. Behind him thundered a heavy-set man who wore a leather apron over brown homespun clothes. With his head down and his thick shoulders thrust forward, he reminded Homan of a bull.

The little man looked back over his shoulder and increased his speed, but to no avail. In a few paces his pursuer overtook him and knocked him to the ground with one powerful blow.

Homan ran forward. Here was a clear case of injustice. A huge bully was beating up a little man and the victim was wearing the uniform of the United States army!

"Leave him alone!" shouted Homan.

The leather aproned man looked up with a surprised expression on his broad face. "You keep out of this," he growled.

Homan planted himself in front of the big man. "Why did you knock him down?"

The little soldier, taking advantage of this diversion, scrambled to his feet and headed up the River Road.

"Out of my way, blockhead!" the other man shouted. His arms flayed the air like windmills and one of them struck Homan full in the face, knocking him flat in the snow. Then the man ran off after the soldier. At this point, the dog went into action, apparently deciding his new friend had been attacked. In spite of his injured foot, he raced up the road after the big fellow.

Homan sat up and applied snow to his nose, which was bleeding profusely. What a powerful brute that man was!

Before long the dog limped back and deposited at Homan's feet a piece of brown homespun. He wagged his tail and looked up with a great air of pride.

"Good dog." Homan patted him approvingly. "I think we saved that little soldier from a beating." Both men had disappeared, but Homan was quite sure the smaller man had had enough of a head start to escape.

Buoyed up by his adventure, Homan no longer hesitated to enter the fort. He thudded across the drawbridge with the dog at his side. U. S. 1462820

When the sentry demanded the password, Homan answered confidently, "Remember the Chesapeake!" That was a good password, he thought. The American people had never forgotten or forgiven the British attack on the United States frigate, *Chesapeake*, in 1807, long before the two countries were at war.

The sentry stepped briskly aside, allowing Homan and the dog to pass through the stone gatehouse. Beyond the gatehouse, the road led a few yards to the north and then plunged into the gloom of a tunnellike blockhouse. This was a solidly built stone structure with barred windows, topped by a square wooden roof. Peering from under the edge of the roof were the muzzles of cannons. The few blue-coated soldiers inside the blockhouse merely glanced at Homan and went back to cleaning their weapons and talking with one another.

As he emerged from the far side of the blockhouse, he squinted in the glare of the snowy parade ground. Where in this busy, noisy place would he find Matt Pomeroy? So many log buildings and tents dotted the field that he didn't know where to start looking. He knew that some of the small buildings were artificers' huts where articles needed by the army were made. There was a blacksmith's hut where the horses were shod, a building where guns were repaired, and a wheel-wright's shop where metal rims were put on wheels. There was a carpenter's hut, too, and a bakehouse.

The huge stone building at the far end of the enclosure was, Homan knew, called the Mess House, and he knew, too, that it was used also as the headquarters for the officers of the fort. Probably that was where he should go to enlist, but first he wanted to find his friend. Perhaps they could arrange to be together in the same company.

Horses neighed in the stable on his left, and he heard the clang of hammer on anvil coming from one of the log build-ings. Fifteen or twenty soldiers, dressed in smart red or green jackets, marched and wheeled on the parade ground, accom-panied by a fife and drum. Their leader glanced toward Homan and issued an order he could not hear. At once the line of marchers turned and came directly toward the block-house. Homan backed up until he was against the cold stone. To his amazement the little dog sat up on his haunches with his paws folded while the marchers crossed back and forth in front of him. Every man in the line was grinning. Finally the leader called a halt. The music stopped; the dog returned to all fours and ran forward to be patted by the soldiers.

"Hey, Shorty, where've you been?" one of them asked affec-tionately. "We've been looking for you all morning."

Another soldier exclaimed in alarm, "Look at him. His foot's hurt!"

The drummer, who appeared to be not over twelve or thir-teen, turned accusingly to Homan. "What happened to Shorty's foot?"

Homan joined the crowd around the dog. "He was caught

in a trap. I found him in the woods, not half an hour ago."

At the sound of Homan's voice, the dog returned to him and jumped up joyfully.

"Guess he's telling the truth," commented the drummer. "You can see Shorty likes him."

"So that's his name," said Homan. He had been called Shorty, himself, more than once, and he hadn't liked it.

"Suits him," the fifer said. "He's our mascot, he is. Been staying around the fort more than a month now. Isn't a man in Fort Niagara but what would share his victuals with Shorty."

"I'll wager he's hungry now," said Homan.

"To the Mess House with him!" One of the soldiers picked up the little dog and ran toward the big stone building.

The drummer said to Homan, "Like as not he'd have died if you hadn't set him free." He made a deep bow, somewhat hampered by his drum. "At your service, sir."

Homan smiled and returned the bow. "Homan Reed. Come to enlist. But first I'd like to find my old friend, Matt Pomeroy."

"Matt!" exclaimed one of the marchers. "He'd be in the kitchen."

"No," another objected. "I saw him only minutes ago, standing in the crowd over there gaping across at Newark. Come on. We'll find him for you."

The friendly group swept Homan toward the western ramparts, where he noticed a solid line of soldiers, all watching the Canadian shore.

Even from the rear, it was easy to pick out Matt. Tall and rangy, with a shock of straw-blond hair, he towered over most of his companions.

Homan tapped him on the shoulder, and Matt whirled

around. A grin spread across his face and he pounded his friend on the back. "Homan! What brings you here?"

"I aim to join up."

"Capital!"

Homan peered around Matt. "What's so interesting over there?"

Matt turned back to the ramparts. "Something peculiar is going on. The townspeople seem to be moving out."

At first Homan saw only the blowing snow and the neat, snow-topped houses set in an orderly fashion along broad streets. The spires of two churches, St. Andrew's and St. Mark's, rose above the trees. Newark was like a New England town. The houses were not log cabins as were most of the homes in Lewiston and Youngstown, but were built of stone or brick or wood.

Before the war, he, Guy, and Uncle Oliver had often rowed across the river to attend church or to shop in the Newark stores. The officers at Fort Niagara had been good friends with the garrison at Fort George. They had gone back and forth to parties and dances, but all of that was changed now. It seemed unfair that a declaration of war in far-off Washington had been able to turn friends into enemies overnight.

As he continued to stare across at the village, Homan saw that furniture was piled in the street outside many of the homes. People hurried in and out of houses or sat on the stacked furniture as if unaware of the snow and cold. Here and there a wagon or sled loaded with household goods moved up a street, headed for the outskirts of the little town.

Homan turned to Matt. "Why are they leaving—and on such a day?"

"I'm not sure. We think General McClure sent word for them to vacate. He's at Fort George, you know."

Homan glanced to the left where he could see the American flag above Fort George on the opposite bank of the river, just south of Newark.

Matt leaned closer to Homan. "Is that blood on your face?"

Homan raised his hand to his face. "It may be. Shorty and I taught a big buzzard some manners. At least we tried to." He told Matt how he had found the dog and then how they both had intervened to save the little soldier.

"Come on," said Matt. "Let's go to the barracks and clean you up before I take you to headquarters to sign up."

As they walked toward a one-story log building on the opposite side of the enclosure, Matt said, "I think I know the fellow who knocked you down. Does he have a flattened nose?"

"Yes!"

Matt sighed and put his hand on Homan's shoulder. "You couldn't have chosen a worse man to pick on than Zeb Humel."

"I didn't pick on him!" Homan protested. "He was beating up a soldier, a much smaller chap! It gave me the whim-whams."

"You always did have the heart of a lion," said Matt with a smile.

"And the size of a mouse," Homan said ruefully.

Matt looked worried. "The trouble is that Zeb is as strong as an ox, and I'm afraid he won't forget you got in his way. Besides, he's a friend of all the officers. He's a fine gunsmith and they like him because he keeps their pistols and muskets in good order. You'll be wise to stay out of his sight."

Homan said gloomily, "I've only just arrived and already I've made an enemy."

"And at least one friend." Matt pointed to Shorty, who was following along at Homan's heels.

Chapter 5

Village in Flames

After the cold of the windswept parade ground, the drafty barracks seemed comfortable. Flames leaped high in two of its four fireplaces.

Homan glanced curiously around the long room. On the east-west walls were wooden bunks, like large trays, filled with straw. The one on Homan's right was occupied by three soldiers, all snoring mightily.

Five or six soldiers dressed in jackets and trousers of blue, drab, or gray lounged in front of a fireplace at the far end of the room. They seemed to be playing a game, for as Homan and Matt entered, a handsome, brown-haired young fellow threw a dagger that bit into the wooden floor with a thud.

One of the soldiers cried out, "Well done, Wilber!" He

leaped forward to pull the dagger loose, and then he himself took careful aim at a circle on the pock-marked floor.

Shorty headed for the nearest fireplace and lay down with his head on his paws. Homan knelt beside him and examined the paw that had been in the trap. The dog took the inspection patiently. He looked up with friendly brown eyes and gave Homan a wet kiss on the chin.

Matt placed a basin of water and a clean rag on a stool beside the fireplace and sat down on a bench while Homan washed the blood from his own face and dressed the dog's sore paw.

"There are only two barracks in the fort that aren't jam-packed with supplies," Matt remarked. "You noticed the tents?"

Homan nodded.

"Men have to sleep in them in this weather," Matt went on. "And they don't like it. I'll try to get you in here with me—though sometimes I sleep in the kitchen. It's quieter there, and warmer, too." He lowered his voice. "You should see the muskets packed away—hundreds and hundreds of 'em! And food! With the vegetables and dried and smoked meats we have in the cellar at the Mess House we could live in that building through a year's seige. We'd even have drinking water."

"Water!" Homan said with a laugh. "With the river on one side and Lake Ontario on another, that would never be a problem."

"If the British had ships on the lake and river you wouldn't find it so simple to fetch a bucketful of water."

"Oh—you're right."

"But don't worry," Matt went on. "We have a well inside

the Mess House in the entrance hall. It's been there ever since the French built the place nigh on a hundred years ago."

"I've seen it. I was inside the Mess House once when I first came to live with Uncle Oliver. I don't recollect much about the building except that well." Homan squinted his eyes, remembering. "It was black and deep. When I leaned over the edge of the stone curb I couldn't see a thing, but when a soldier lowered a bucket I heard it splash and it came up full of water. I was only eleven then, and I thought, What if someone fell in there at night?"

Matt smiled at Homan. "That reminds me of a tale I heard. It seems two French officers fought a duel over an Indian maid, and the winner cut off the head of the other fellow. He threw the body down the well but tossed the head into Lake Ontario. 'Tis said a headless ghost haunts the Mess House at night and wanders up and down looking for its head."

Homan shuddered. "Have you seen the ghost?"

"We-ll," said Matt. "I can't say I have. Nor have I gone searching for it." He looked critically at his friend. "You're getting a nose like a ripe plum."

Homan felt his nose gingerly. "My reward for poking it into other people's business. But I'd do the same thing again. I hope that little soldier escaped." He yawned. The warmth of the fire was making him sleepy and he was tempted to stretch out on the floor like Shorty.

Shorty, he thought. Maybe he'd give him a new name.

Matt picked up the basin of water. "Looks as if you have a dog."

"Who owns him?"

"No one now. He belonged to a family who lived on the lake shore. They figured they were too close to Canada for safety and moved east to Albany, and they left Shorty behind.

He stays around here for the food, I suppose. Everyone feeds him. And every night, regular as clockwork, he comes around to the kitchen for a big plate of scraps I save for him."

"So you're still in the kitchen," said Homan, laughing.

Matt grinned and scratched his head, pushing his cap at a jaunty angle. "Some fellow who'd eaten the victuals I fixed at Hustler's Tavern spoke up and said I was the best cook west of Albany."

Homan nodded approval. "Not even Anne and Molly can make rabbit potpie a whit better than you."

Matt went on, "When I said I'd come to fight the enemy, not cook, I was told it's as important to feed our army as to kill the enemy. I hadn't been here for a month when I was promoted to head cook. It was my experience in cooking for hungry mouths at Hustler's that helped me."

The door at the far end of the barracks crashed open and a young soldier thrust his head into the room long enough to shout, "Our troops are leaving Fort George—with torches!" Everyone in the barracks headed for the door. Even the soldiers who had been sleeping staggered to their feet and followed the others.

The parade ground was alive with hurrying men, all bound for the already crowded western ramparts. Homan, being short, knew he wouldn't have a chance to get a good view. As he looked about for a vantage point, he spied an artificer's hut nearby. An artillery carriage standing against the side of the building gave him an idea. He climbed up on it and from there found it quite easy to pull himself onto the edge of the roof. Making steps for himself in the deeply piled snow, he reached the peak. There, standing beside the chimney, which he held onto, he had an uninterrupted view of the opposite shore.

In Newark people were running around distractedly. Sometimes they would pick up a piece of furniture, carry it a few paces, and then set it down to snatch up a blanket to wrap around a child. Here and there, Homan saw an American soldier helping to carry furniture from the houses. The only Canadian men he could see appeared even at this distance to be elderly. Women and children made up the rest of the population. No doubt the younger men were in the army. Occasionally a sound carried across the river—a shout, the loud wail of a baby, or the sharp bark of a dog.

From the foot of the hut where he was standing, Matt Pomeroy called, "Hey up there! Homan!" He waved a spyglass over his head.

"Come on up!"

"How'd you get there?"

"Go around to the side. Climb on the gun carriage."

A moment later, Matt clambered onto the roof, making the entire building shake.

"Great lookout post!" he exclaimed. Bracing himself against the chimney, he trained the spyglass on the village across the river.

A shout from the ramparts made both boys look upriver. There, on the opposite bank, Homan could now see a long, advancing line of soldiers in blue. Many of the marchers carried lighted torches and lanterns. The first groups of soldiers entered the outskirts of the village. Within a few minutes, Homan could see the blue-uniformed men moving about all over the town. The people began to hurry to the fields to the south and west of the village.

"Fire!" cried one of the men on the ramparts of Fort Niagara.

At almost the same moment, a wail sounded from the people of Newark. A flame shot up from a house near the waterfront. A moment later a house on the next street was ablaze. Homan watched in fascination and horror as flames appeared on every street.

A wave of angry muttering rose from the ramparts.

"Why are they burning the houses?" Homan asked.

"Because McClure is a fool!" Matt answered without lowering the telescope.

"*Our* General McClure? The one who's in charge at Fort George?"

Matt pointed to the line of soldiers that was still pouring into the village. "It looks as if *our* General McClure and all his men have left Fort George."

Homan felt bewildered. American soldiers didn't burn peoples' houses—not without a good reason. What could be the reason for turning these women and children and old men out into the winter weather? He couldn't see a British uniform or a Mohawk on the opposite shore. And Guy was over there. Was he burning houses, too?

"Look there!" he exclaimed, shaking Matt's arm. He pointed to a street near the south end of town where three people were carrying what appeared to be a bed down a short flight of steps from a porch. "Is someone in that bed?"

Matt shoved the spyglass into Homan's hand. "Here, look for yourself."

The narrow bed *was* occupied, Homan discovered. It was being moved with great care by a woman and two children. Three blue-coated soldiers stood by. One wore the epaulets and sash of an officer. "Why don't they help?" cried Homan.

As if in response, one of the soldiers thrust his torch into a snowbank and took the foot of the cot from the unsteady hands of the children. The officer stepped forward as if to object, but the other soldier pushed past him and seized the head of the cot. The officer shrugged his shoulders and walked away. The little procession moved slowly up the street led by the two children. Wind lifted the blankets and the woman hurried to tuck them more securely around the invalid.

Carrying that bed—that was the kind of thing Guy would do. But even with the aid of the spyglass Homan could not identify the helpful soldiers. As the cot rounded the corner of the street, another group of soldiers with torches set fire to the house from which the invalid had been carried.

"That's terrible!" said Homan. "How could they put a sick person out on a day like this!" In his excitement he forgot his slippery perch and started away from the chimney. He lost his footing and would have fallen if Matt had not seized his arm.

"Gently there!" said Matt, helping him back to the chimney. "I don't like what's happening over there, either, but we can't stop it. This is war."

"War or not, I know Guy isn't setting fire to those houses!" Homan returned the spyglass to Matt.

"You don't know what you're talking about." Matt sounded irritated. "Wait till you're in the army and you'll find out that you do what you're told—or else!" Matt's eyes were on the Canadian shore, and now he raised the spyglass excitedly. "Maybe you can ask Guy, himself, what he's been doing." He nodded toward Newark where soldiers were crowding onto the docks and rapidly boarding the boats that were lined up there. The first boat pushed off and started across the river. Homan could see the bend and lift of the men at the oars as they pulled across the mouth of the river toward Fort Niagara. Matt groaned, "We'll have to feed that crowd!"

The watchers on the ramparts were shouting angrily at the oncoming boat. "Shame!" "Why did you burn the town?" "Go back!" Some soldiers even ran down to the dock with the clear intention of preventing the boat from landing. An officer strode after them, gave a sharp command, and they fell back.

"That's Captain Leonard," Matt explained. "He's Captain of the Artillery and in command of this fort. A regular martinet he is. And a taskmaster—insists on two hours of cannon practice every day."

The first boat docked and the soldiers started through Trader Town and up the slope toward the fort. Two other boats were on the way across the river, and the first was returning for another load of men. There were only three boats in all.

Fanned by the strong wind which had shifted to the west, the flames of the burning village now soared to the sky. Ashes and red embers rained onto the dock and the soldiers waiting their turn to cross. Even here at Fort Niagara, smoke and ashes billowed over the heads of the men on the ramparts and the two on the roof of the artificer's shack. The acrid smoke made Homan's eyes water.

The angry murmurs of the watchers now rose to a roar. Homan peered down, looking for an explanation of this, and saw an officer coming up the path from the dock to the narrow western gate.

"That's McClure!" cried a soldier on the ramparts. "Shoot him!"

From many throats came angry cries. "Blackguard!" "Villain!" "Now you've done it! It'll be our turn tomorrow!"

Startled, Homan turned to Matt, who seemed to understand Homan's unspoken question. "They're right," he said. "The British will want revenge for this day's work. They'll put American homes to the torch as soon as they're able."

Chapter 6

Is Guy a Tory?

As Brigadier General McClure entered Fort Niagara through the western gate, the soldiers inside surged toward him, shouting threats and abuse. For a moment it looked as if he might be crushed, but the soldiers who had crossed from Newark with him formed a wedge-shaped line of protection around him. Close behind came Captain Leonard, guarding the General from rear attack.

Matt said hastily, "I'm leaving while the way is clear. You'll find me in the kitchen!" He slid down the roof in a flurry of snow.

Left alone, Homan watched McClure's angry red face and heard him roar at the mob to fall back and let him through. The officers in the fort did their best to restrain their men, but the crowd followed all the way across the parade ground and up to the solid stone walls of the Mess House. Even after General McClure had disappeared inside, the excited soldiers continued to shout and mill about. Several fist fights broke out between McClure's men and those from Fort Niagara.

Homan heard one of the newcomers shout, "We were only obeying orders! We didn't *want* to do it!"

This was what Matt had said. Soldiers had to obey their officers.

Glancing back toward Newark, Homan saw several sleighs drawn up to the south of the village where some of the refugees had gathered. People and household goods were being loaded on the sleighs. He was glad to see that Canadians from the nearby countryside were rallying to help the unfortunate citizens of Newark.

The dock across the river was empty of soldiers and the three boats that had been used to carry McClure's men across were fastened at the docks of Trader Town. That must mean all of the American forces from Fort George were now at Fort Niagara.

Eagerly Homan turned this way and that to scan the crowds below him for the sight of his brother's handsome head. But it was not possible to pick out any one man with so many wearing similar uniforms. Perhaps if he were on the ground with the others he would have better luck. Up here he had a long view, but he saw mostly the tops of heads.

Strange, he thought. When I'm with Guy we often disagree and I think I can get along very well without him. But when we're apart I only remember the good times we've had and I can't wait to see him again.

Imitating Matt's descent from the roof, Homan landed on his feet in the snow. With his musket at his side, he pushed his way through the men who thronged the parade ground. Here and there groups were warming their hands over small fires. Homan looked into all of the faces. He ducked inside the bakehouse and then spent a few minutes in the chapel, tiptoeing up and down the aisles in the hope of seeing his brother among the soldiers who had come in to pray or perhaps just to get warm. Outside again, he came to the blacksmith's hut, but gave it a wide berth. Zeb Humel might be back at work now, and Homan had no desire to meet him again.

He asked a passing soldier, "Do you know Guy Reed?" and was met with a blank stare. The next man he questioned answered, "If he's from across the river, I wouldn't know him. I've been right here all along."

Becoming bolder, Homan thrust his head inside a small tent and asked, "Has anyone seen Guy Reed?"

After a moment of silence, several of the soldiers laughed. One asked, "What do you want him for?"

"He's my brother."

Again there was laughter, but just as Homan was about to retreat, one of the men lifted his hand with a gesture that silenced the others. He fixed Homan with a threatening stare.

"Are you a Tory like your brother?"

"He's not a Tory!" Homan exclaimed. "And neither am I! I've just come here to enlist."

Several men snickered, but the one who had questioned Homan turned to them and said sharply, "He's serious—can't you see?" To Homan he added gravely, "Don't tell anyone your name is Reed if you sign up. Like as not they'll stake you out for the Indians!"

"Why?" asked Homan in alarm.

"Never you mind why," the man said. "Your brother's decided to stay in Canada. Now begone!"

Bewildered, Homan dragged himself back to the western

ramparts. It was now very dark and smoke was still drifting over from Newark. Inside the walls of the fort, flares and campfires made patches of light but added to the haze. He was worried and he needed time to think. Guy was no Tory, even though he had never been in favor of the war. Had he sickened of it and deserted? Or were those men lying?

Tired and cold, Homan sat down at the foot of the ramparts, close to a gun emplacement. Several soldiers were clustered around a small fire. Unlike most of the crowd on the parade ground, these men were deep in a serious discussion. A slim soldier with his back to Homan had brown hair the color of Guy's. It was longer than Guy's when he had last seen him, but six months had passed since then—plenty of time for hair to grow. Besides, there was something familiar about the set of the man's shoulders. With rising hope, Homan moved closer.

But it was not Guy. As the man turned sideways, Homan recognized the good-looking young soldier called Wilber whom he had seen playing the game with the dagger in the barracks.

"Newark's burned to a crisp, whether we like it or not," Wilber was saying. "I don't think President Madison will like it when he hears about it, but nothing he can do now will save us. You can be sure the British are already planning to get even for *that.*" He jerked his head toward Canada where flames still shot skyward.

"Let them try," another soldier said confidently. "They'll never be able to take Fort Niagara."

Homan silently agreed. This was a real stronghold. Besides being protected on one side by the lake and the other by the river, it was completely surrounded by walls of earth and a sharp picket stockade. Even if the enemy managed to get inside the enclosure, they'd never take the blockhouses that guarded the north and south ends of the fort. Nor could they break into the stone Mess House where even now Brigadier General McClure, Captain Leonard, and the other officers were having a conference. Why, those walls must be more than two feet thick. Uncle Oliver had told him it had stood there ever since 1726 when the Frenchman, Joncaire, had arranged for it to be built. Joncaire had told the Seneca Indians, who had owned the land then, that he wanted to build a strong trading house. They wouldn't have allowed a fort to be built, but since they liked Joncaire, they had permitted the French engineers to erect the big stone building for a trading post. Too late, the Indians found out they had been tricked, and that Joncaire's trading house was an impregnable fortress with loopholes for guns and walls no cannon—let alone arrows—could penetrate.

To Homan's surprise, Wilber said, "What makes you so sure this fort can't be taken? The British won it from the French back in the French and Indian War. It took a long siege, but they starved out Captain Pouchot and his men."

"Haw!" said one of the soldiers. "They'd have a hard time starving us out with all the food we have stored up."

"You're right there," conceded Wilber. "And the fort is stronger than when Pouchot was here. We have the British to thank for that." He paused. "But even if they can't take the fort away from us, what's to stop them from burning Lewiston and Manchester? They have right smart officers, even though they did lose General Brock in the Queenstown battle. They'll collect an army and come over here, as sure as my name's Wilber Shaw."

"Yer dead right!" called out the soldier who was manning

the cannon nearby. "And it's McClure we have to thank for it! He's run off and left Fort George for the British to help themselves to, after all our trouble capturing it."

Homan felt his dislike for McClure increasing. If Lewiston were burned, his own cabin was likely to go up in flames with all the rest. And Anne, Molly, and Jeremy would be put out in the snow like the people of Newark.

"McClure's not all to blame," spoke up a soldier who had come unnoticed onto the ramparts to the north of the group. "I was over there in Fort George and I can tell you we couldn't have held that fort another day."

"Why not?" demanded Wilber.

"Because the term was up for most of the militia and they went home. There were about four hundred volunteers a couple of weeks ago and today we were down to forty, with only about sixty regulars. Then we got the word that Colonel Murray was marching on us, and believe me, we were glad McClure decided to give up the fort. If we'd waited much longer, we wouldn't get across, for floating ice in the river."

"All right," said Wilber. "But why did you burn Newark?"

The soldier who had been with McClure put his gloved hands to his ears. "My ears are froze, I reckon—and all that heat over there going to waste."

No one laughed at his attempt to distract them, so he went on. "All right, I'll tell you why we burned Newark. It was so the British couldn't use the houses for barracks."

Wilber cocked his head to one side. "And I suppose you burned the barracks and tents at Fort George so they couldn't use them, either?"

"Well, no," McClure's soldier admitted. "We came away too fast."

Wilber groaned. "You couldn't burn the barracks, but you had all the time in the world to burn the whole bloomin' town."

Homan was so interested in the conversation that he didn't notice the approach of the small black dog until the little fellow greeted him with a joyful bark. Lonely and worried as he was, Homan felt as if Shorty were an old friend. He pulled him close. "Did I leave you in the barracks?" he asked contritely.

One of the men grouped around the fire sang out, "Looks as if Shorty's found his owner. Say, young fellow, does that dog belong to you?"

"No. I never saw him before today." He rubbed the dog's head. "He's a fine dog. I wish he were mine."

Wilber walked over to stand in front of Homan. He reached down and patted the dog. "Shorty seems to feel the same way about you. Why don't you take him home with you?"

"I'm not going home. I came here to enlist."

"Enlist!" cried Wilber. "Stand up, boy, and let me look you over." The other soldiers left the cannon and joined Wilber.

Homan got to his feet. Let them make fun of him!

Wilber looked him up and down, but his voice was kind as he said, "Why do you want to enlist, little fellow? You don't have the size for a soldier."

"I can shoot as well as anyone," Homan said with dignity. Why must people always judge by size?

"This war isn't just shooting," said Wilber. "A good deal of it is hand-to-hand fighting. Suppose the Indians ambush you? You'll get one good shot with your musket and then they'll be on top of you. No time for you to reload, so you have to fight back with your bayonet and your hunting knife. That's where you'd be in trouble. You don't have the reach. You'd be a casualty in the first engagement."

Homan's face was red. "You might give me a chance to prove what I can do before you bury me." He picked up his musket and stalked away with the dog at his heels.

Behind him he heard one of the men say, "The gun's bigger than he is!"

This remark was followed by laughter, but Homan kept his head up and strode on. He'd show them. He'd show everyone!

Chapter 7

Arrival at Night

Homan was hungry and almost exhausted, but he clung stubbornly to one idea. He had come here to enlist, and somehow he was going to add his name to the muster roll before morning.

With this in mind, he plodded across the snowy parade ground toward the Mess House. Most of the soldiers had withdrawn to their tents to await the late mess call. Homan experienced a feeling of awe as the Mess House loomed up before him—two stories high and topped by an open gun deck. The stone front was lighted up by rows of flaring torches set in the snow. All of the windows on the first floor were barred and the gun deck was encircled by a stout, notched wall like the battlements of a castle. In the openings,

Homan could see the snouts of cannons. Tall chimneys, towering above the gun deck, gave evidence of several fireplaces within. Years ago the trappers and traders had called the building "The Castle," and that seemed a more appropriate name for this imposing structure.

Homan knocked boldly on the thick oaken door.

A voice called out, "Who goes there?"

Did he dare identify himself as Guy Reed's brother? He squared his shoulders defiantly. He'd not enter the army under a false name. "Homan Reed from Lewiston!"

"What do you want?" There was no recognition in the sentry's voice.

Still smarting from the laughter of Wilber and his companions, Homan fairly shouted, "I want to enlist!"

"You can't. All the officers are in conference," said the invisible sentry.

"Then I'll see the cook, Matt Pomeroy!" If he could get inside the Mess House, he could look for an officer when the conference was over. In the meantime, he knew Matt would give him something to eat.

"Present yourself," said the voice.

At first Homan did not know what he was supposed to do. Then he noticed a small barred window set in the door, high above his head.

"I can't reach the window," he admitted, with some embarrassment, though he was consoled by the fact that there were few men whose eyes would be on a level with that opening.

"Pull yourself up, blockhead!" said the voice from within.

Homan rested his musket against the doorway, and reaching up seized the bars and lifted himself until his head was in front of the window. Smart planning, he thought with admiration. If an enemy were trying to get in, he'd have to put his weapon down before he could show his face.

"You look harmless enough." There was amusement in the sentry's voice.

Homan dropped to the ground and retrieved his gun as the door swung silently open on well-greased iron hinges. He scurried inside, followed by Shorty, and the door closed behind him just as silently.

The entrance hall was deserted except for the sentry who, with complete indifference, had turned his back. Homan looked around, trying to guess the location of the kitchen. To his left, the door was open to a firelit room with a long, slanting bunk built against the right-hand wall. At the end of the bunk, he could see a rack where several muskets were standing. The room was crowded with soldiers lounging on the bunk or in front of the fireplace. The room on his right was the trading center. In spite of the dim light, Homan could see a long counter. Beside it were scales, hanging from a rafter. On shelves behind the counter were bolts of cloth, two or three muskets, and an untidy stack of pelts. Someone stood up behind the counter and Homan started toward the trade room, planning to ask the direction of the kitchen.

But Shorty had other ideas. He trotted straight ahead underneath a massive stone archway and then turned to the right. Homan, following him, realized that this was the direction from which tantalizing odors were coming. At the end of the short corridor was the kitchen.

The room was full of cooks in aprons and soldiers with towels wrapped around their waists to protect their uniforms, but only a few of these men were actually at work. Most of them lounged on benches or against the tables, talking loudly and getting in the way of the workers.

Candles flickered on the mantel, on the long table at the left of the fireplace, and in wall brackets alongside the shelves that lined the room. A lantern hung from a blackened beam.

Matt was adjusting an already well-browned side of pork on a rack of hooks that he swung over the fire. He saw Shorty first and said wearily, "Supper's late for you and everyone else. Too many mouths to feed tonight." He poked in a kettle and fished out a morsel of meat with a fork. He blew on it and tested it with his fingers before he tossed it to Shorty. "There, how's that for a sample?"

Shorty swallowed the meat in one gulp.

Homan, standing in the doorway, was almost bowled over by a soldier who pushed in behind him and demanded to know when supper would be ready.

"Officers first," Matt replied curtly. "We'll let you know."

Homan leaned wearily against the wall. The good smell of food and the warmth of the room took him back more than three years to the kitchen at home in Connecticut. He remembered how, when he got back from school, his mother sometimes gave him a thick slice of bread warm from the oven.

Matt called out, "Homan, will you give me a hand? Come over here and stir this stew."

Homan set his musket and pack against the wall and joined his friend at the stone fireplace. Grease dripping from the pork made the fire hiss and crackle.

"I have all those extra mouths to feed," Matt grumbled, "and for helpers they give me numskulls with two left hands apiece."

For the next half-hour Homan was kept busy.

"At least you have the sense to follow directions," Matt commented. "I'd make a cook out of you in no time."

"I've been fixing my own victuals ever since Guy left," Homan told him.

At last Matt wiped his face on his sleeve and announced that supper was ready.

He handed Homan a stack of plates and a fresh loaf of bread. "You carry these, and I'll bring the meat." He had the choicest loin of pork on a board, ready for carving.

A small procession went down the hall from the kitchen to the first door on the right. A kitchen boy was in the lead with a tray of glasses and cutlery. Not since he had left New England had Homan seen such fine glassware.

As they entered the paneled conference room, the officers got to their feet with exclamations of "Food at last!" They scooped papers from the much-stained, oaken table so it could be set, and then walked about, stretching and talking in low tones to each other. Homan recognized Brigadier General McClure and Captain Leonard still seated side by side at the head of the long table.

Homan hurried about, helping to set the table and cutting the crusty bread, fresh from the bakehouse. As he worked, he kept his ears open. He had no trouble hearing McClure's loud voice.

"They might even come over tonight," he was saying. "Colonel Murray was pulling close when I left Fort George."

Captain Leonard asked a question Homan couldn't hear, but McClure's reply filled every corner of the long room. "If they don't come tonight, they'll be here the next. I'll leave you with four hundred men altogether and I'll put about forty along the river between here and Buffalo."

"Forty!" Captain Leonard cried. "How can forty men protect more than thirty miles of frontier?"

"They'll manage," said McClure. "There are men at Fort Gray and at Fort Schlosser now. The important spot is right here. Keep this place and we have the route inland under control. Fort Niagara is the gateway. As long as we hold it, boats can't get past here to go up the river or get to the portage around the falls."

Uncle Oliver used to say, "If you have something worth saying, you don't have to shout it." Why was McClure making such a big noise about Fort Niagara? Surely, Captain Leonard didn't need to be told it was an important post.

Matt carved the meat, and immediately the officers fell to like starved men. Homan lingered near the table, wondering if he dared ask Captain Leonard to sign him up, but Matt signaled to him from the door.

"Come on," he urged. "We'll grab something to eat, and then we have a hungry army to feed."

It was past midnight before Homan was finished in the kitchen. Then he was so tired he was glad to drop onto a bench beside the fireplace where Matt had spread a blanket for him. Shorty was already asleep on a bearskin rug before the fire. Beside his bench, Homan placed his musket, in case the English attacked during the night—though of course they'd never get within these walls. In the morning, come what might, he'd enlist. Hard as his bed was, he fell asleep at once.

Three hours later he was suddenly awakened. Someone was shaking his shoulder. The enemy has attacked! he thought. But when he opened his eyes to the dimly lighted room, he saw Guy bending over him. Matt was standing beside him with a candle in his hand, and Shorty was looking on anxiously as if wondering whether he should chase off this stranger who had awakened his new master.

"Guy!" Homan flung himself off the bench.

"Hush, lad!" Guy drew him close for a brief hug. Then he pushed him down onto the bench and sat beside him.

Matt placed his candle on the nearby table and took a loaf of bread from the cupboard.

"You have to leave right away," Guy said in an urgent whisper. "The English may be here before morning."

"Leave? Never!" exclaimed Homan, forgetting to be quiet. "I'm enlisting!"

Guy laid his hand over Homan's mouth. "Don't wake the entire army," he whispered. "Now, listen to me. I just came across the river and I know this for truth. Colonel Murray's camped right outside Newark. As soon as he can, he'll be over here."

"Why didn't you come here with the others?" demanded Homan.

"I stayed to help some refugees—old friends of Uncle Oliver's," Guy said hurriedly. "One of them rowed me across, at great danger to himself, not half an hour ago."

"McClure's men said you deserted!" Homan blurted out.

"I had no such intention," said Guy. "I'll fight for my country till I die, but I won't take part in burning the houses of innocent women and children!" His eyes flashed indignantly. "I'm not the only one who objected to the burning of Newark. A goodly part of the men felt as I did. Colonel Chapin from Buffalo was against it, too. He and McClure were in the sutler's store on Queen Street in Newark yesterday, arguing about it. I heard them with my own ears."

To his own surprise, Homan found himself agreeing wholeheartedly with Guy. "I'd have done the same as you," he admitted.

Guy laughed with delight. "Don't tell me our War Hawk is turning into a dove of peace!"

Matt laid out a slice of bread and a generous slab of cold pork. "I hear you're in McClure's bad graces," he remarked.

"I don't doubt it," Guy answered. "I'll be lucky if I don't have to face a court-martial, but I don't regret what I did." He waved the food aside. "Later. Right now we have to start Homan on his way."

"I'm not going!" declared Homan. The moment of accord was gone.

Guy drew a deep breath, obviously struggling to keep his temper. "Youngstown and Lewiston are in grave danger," he said. "You must go to warn them, and then help the Warrens to escape."

Homan said stubbornly, "You go. I'm not leaving just so I can take care of your girl."

"I can't leave! I *would* be a deserter then!" Guy exploded. He added more quietly, "It's true I love Anne. We plan to marry when the war is over. But it isn't just Anne I'm thinking of now."

Homan was speechless. He had known Guy liked Anne but had not guessed that they were betrothed.

Guy continued, "Now, when you get there, harness the oxen to the sled and load on everything you can in a hurry. Anything you leave will be burned. That's what Murray's planning."

"What about our place?" Homan demanded.

"Oh!" It was plain that Guy had not even thought of that. "Well, take along whatever you can carry. But don't worry about *things*. Just get away with your lives. Now, go!"

"But Mr. Warren——" began Homan.

"He's at Fort Gray, and after what happened today, he'll have no time to help his family."

"Oh, all right!" Homan pulled on his coat, picked up his gun, and retrieved the shoulder pack he had laid beside the fireplace. Musket in hand, he stood in the middle of the kitchen. "I'll be back as soon as I get Anne, Molly, and Jeremy on their way," he informed his brother.

"Enough talk!" Guy beckoned him toward the door. "Get them started east on the Ridge Road. They have an aunt in Batavia who'll take them in, I believe."

Matt joined the two brothers. He thrust some bread and meat into Homan's pack. "We'll see you to the gate."

Chapter 8

Zeb Takes the Canoe

The cold air almost took Homan's breath away. As he, Shorty, Guy, and Matt crossed the parade ground past the silent tents and log buildings, the snow crunched under their feet.

At the gate Matt gave the password. "Remember that," he cautioned Homan. "You'll need it if you run into any sentries along the way."

The soldier at the gate demanded, "Name!"

To Matt and Homan he merely nodded and let them pass, but when Guy gave his name, the sentry's manner changed. "You're under arrest!" he snapped.

"What for?" asked Guy.

"General McClure's orders!" The sentry called another soldier. "Lock this man up."

Guy reached for his brother's hand. "God go with you."

Homan didn't move. "I'm not going to leave you, Guy!"

"There's nothing you can do," Guy said impatiently. "Go!"

Matt tugged at Homan's arm. "Come. He's right. You can't help him by staying. I'll look after him. I'm in Captain Leonard's good graces."

Torn by indecision, Homan allowed Matt to lead him through the gate. Looking back over his shoulder, he saw his brother with a guard on either side headed back across the parade ground toward the Mess House.

"Don't let them lock him up!" Homan begged. He couldn't bear to think of Guy imprisoned, especially at the fort. Though he had never seen the jail at Fort Niagara, he had heard that it was a cold and cheerless place. Even worse than the jail was the dungeon—a windowless stone cell used for solitary confinement. Men who were locked there went mad from utter loneliness. What if McClure were angry enough to send Guy there?

He pushed Matt toward the gate. "Stop them!"

"I'll try my best," Matt promised. "And you—if you see the enemy, skirt around them and keep going!"

Homan, with Shorty trotting briskly ahead of him, crossed the drawbridge and walked swiftly down the road without another backward glance. He was sure if he looked back, he would be tempted to return, and reason told him Matt and Guy were right. What could he accomplish by returning? At least by going to Lewiston he could save some of their belongings and put Guy's mind at ease about the safety of the Warrens—and his own mind, as well. Guy was right. He must get Molly and her brother and sister away from Lewiston.

At first his mind was so intent on Guy that he saw nothing as he strode along. Then gradually he became aware of the cold wind on his face. He began to notice the white, empty road, edged by trees that were black against the snow. Here the road was near the river bank and he could see the orange of several small fires on the opposite shore south of Newark. Were those the campfires of the enemy Guy said were gathering to attack Fort Niagara? Perhaps even now they were preparing to cross the river. "Heaven help us if they come over tonight," he said to Shorty.

He strode to the cliff that rose above the shore and stared earnestly up and down the river. No boats were within sight on or near the water and there seemed to be no unusual activity on the Canadian side. Reassured, Homan continued his lonely journey.

The road was deserted until he reached Youngstown, almost a mile away. There in front of Campbell's Tavern he came upon a sentry stamping up and down, swinging his arms. His musket was resting against the tavern wall. When he saw the boy and dog, he made a dive for his gun, but Homan soon put him at ease by giving him the password.

"I hope the enemy won't creep up the quiet way you did," the man said.

"We didn't creep up," Homan objected. "You were making so much noise with your own boots, you wouldn't have heard a whole army."

"Well, I've been out here a long time," the sentry complained. "The rest of the guards are inside playing cards. The loser has to stand watch. They're taking a powerful long time to get another loser."

"You'd better keep a sharp watch," Homan warned him. "The British may attack before daybreak. They want revenge for Newark."

The sentry was not impressed. "Any blockhead knows that. Half the people around here have left already. We went around and alerted them. The ones who stayed said they felt safe enough with the fort close by, and that's my opinion, too."

Had everyone been warned? Homan wondered. It would be like Guy to give him any task just to get him out of danger.

"What about Lewiston?" he asked.

The sentry shrugged. "They must have seen the fire, but our messengers didn't go that far, if that's what you mean."

Homan was half-tempted to return to the fort, but he decided he had better go on. The people of Lewiston might not realize the nearness of danger—and, of course, he still had to start the Warren family on the way to safety.

After passing the Swain house at Bloody Run, a desolate stretch lay ahead and he was glad for the company of Shorty. A bitter wind made the trees sway and creak. Not even a rabbit or a wolf seemed to be abroad tonight, but twice he met sentries on the road, wide-awake and worried by the flames of Newark.

As Homan neared his own cabin, he was startled to see someone dart across the road toward the river and disappear among the trees. Surely that wasn't a sentry! Shorty uttered a low growl. Homan put his hand on the dog's back to quiet him and felt the hair bristling along the animal's spine.

"Quiet!" he whispered. He took shelter among the trees on his right and was relieved when Shorty followed silently and stayed close beside him. The person ahead might be a friend or an enemy, but there was no way of knowing unless they came face to face.

Cautiously he edged forward until he heard the crunch of snow close by. He ducked behind a large oak tree, pulling Shorty with him. For a few moments he waited, afraid that the stranger had heard him. As soon as he dared, he peered around the tree trunk. Only a few feet ahead on the river bank stood a heavy-set man with a musket in the crook of his arm. That chunky figure looked familiar. The man bent to descend the bank, and as he did so, his profile was plain against the snow. The slanting forehead and the flattened nose could belong to only one man—Zeb Humel. What was he doing here?

Shorty growled again.

Zeb turned quickly and stared into the woods. Homan pulled back behind the tree and clamped his hand around the dog's muzzle. After a long pause he heard a scrambling, sliding sound. Zeb must be going down the steep slope to the river. Homan relaxed his hold on Shorty, and the moment he was free, the dog made a wild dash for the river bank and disappeared over the edge.

Homan ran out of the woods and crouched behind a rock at the top of the cliff. Below him and a few yards to the south, Zeb was pulling a canoe—Homan and Dave Cusick's canoe—from beneath the willow tree. With the ease of practice, he flipped it over and carried it down toward the water's edge. Homan felt certain this was not the first time Zeb had taken the canoe.

As Shorty came sliding down the bank, Zeb dropped the canoe and whirled to face the dog with a dagger gleaming in his hand.

Homan knew Zeb Humel was a dangerous man, and already he had good reason to hate Shorty and his new master. The wise thing to do would be to stay out of sight, but he couldn't let Zeb stab Shorty. He gave the rock in front of him a violent shove, hoping to draw the man's attention from the dog. While the rock went bouncing and crashing down the bank and into the river, Homan ran back from the edge of the cliff and with shaking fingers took a cartridge from his pouch. He bit off the twist of paper at the top and shook some of the powder into the pan to prime the gun. The rest of the cartridge he dropped into the muzzle. As quickly as he could, he tamped it down with his ramrod. Now he was ready.

With the musket leveled at the top of the bank he crept forward, expecting Zeb to appear at any moment. Instead, when he reached the cliff, he saw Zeb well out in the river, paddling at top speed toward the opposite shore. Shorty was nowhere in sight.

Homan had a sickening fear that the dog was dead. He raised his musket. Zeb was still within range. He took careful aim, but didn't pull the trigger. Slowly he lowered his gun. He couldn't shoot this man, no matter how much he disliked and distrusted him. Zeb was an American. He might even be valuable to the army, for Matt had said he was an expert at repairing the officers' weapons.

"Shorty!" he called.

He had little hope of any answer, but a friendly bark sounded near the water's edge, and the dog came frisking up the bank. Homan ran down to meet him and lifted him up in his arms. He held him so closely he could feel the rapid beating of Shorty's heart. At that moment he made up his mind not to change Shorty's name. It wouldn't be fair to change a name to which the dog answered so promptly. And being small was nothing for a dog to be ashamed of. He was a brave dog, and that was more important than size.

Together, he and Shorty watched Zeb paddle across the river until he disappeared from sight in the darkness. The man did not once turn to look back. Homan wondered why he was crossing the river by night. Was he on a private mission for the Americans? Or was he deserting?

As he continued toward his cabin, Homan wondered how

Shorty had escaped death. Even if the dog was too quick for the dagger, Zeb could have turned the musket on him. Perhaps he had been afraid of attracting attention by firing his gun. Still, Homan was surprised he hadn't come up to find out who had sent the rock rolling down the steep river bank.

Probably he knew very well who it was, Homan thought with a shiver. Now Zeb had two good reasons for revenge.

Chapter 9

Homan Is Needed

The sky was beginning to turn gray, though dawn was still more than an hour away when Homan reached his cabin. Fresh snow had blotted out all tracks and he sank knee-deep into it as he crossed the clearing. When Shorty plunged out of sight except for the end of his black tail, Homan picked him up and carried him under his arm.

Inside the cabin the air was almost as cold as out, but Homan had no time to start a fire. He took out his tinderbox and struck a flint so he could light a candle. Then he looked around the room, trying to decide what he should save from the destruction that might strike the frontier. He wished he could take the big iron kettle Uncle Oliver had brought from Connecticut and the pine table he and Guy had built, but he had no way to carry them. Finally he decided on an extra shirt and pair of breeches, the copy of *Pilgrim's Progress*, and a pewter teapot that his mother had treasured. He tied these inside a quilt and blew out the candle.

If his plans had worked out, he'd have been getting outfitted at the fort today. Tomorrow he'd go back, he promised himself—just as soon as he got Molly, Anne, and Jeremy started east.

By the time he reached the Warrens', it was daylight and he was staggering with weariness. Anne let him in. Her face bore signs of a sleepless night. He laid down his bundles and musket just inside the door.

Anne turned to look curiously at Shorty, who scurried in, went straight to the hearth, and flopped down.

"That's Shorty," Homan explained. "I rescued him from a trap and he's been following me ever since." He pushed the door shut behind him. "I've just come from Fort Niagara. I saw Guy and he said you have to leave right away. McClure's men have burned Newark, by his orders, and now the British will try to take revenge on Youngstown and likely as not Lewiston, as well." He had decided not to tell Anne of Guy's arrest. It would only add to her worry.

"Oh, no!" Anne moaned. Her eyes darted to the small bed beside the fireplace. "We can't leave. Jeremy's sick and we daren't move him."

Homan came farther into the room and dropped onto a chair by the kitchen table. "What's wrong with him?"

"Dr. Smith says it's fever—maybe typhus."

Homan felt as if he had just received a blow in the stomach. Typhus was a terrible sickness. Of course Jeremy couldn't be moved if that's what he had. But if the enemy came and burned the houses——

"Can I see him?" he asked.

Anne motioned him to follow her to the bed beside the fire-place. "I moved him here to keep him warm," she whispered.

Homan bent over the sleeping child. Jeremy's face was flushed, and even though he slept, his mouth was twisted as if with pain. A hopeless feeling came over Homan as he shuffled back to the chair by the kitchen table. He tried to think what they should do, but the more he thought, the more confused he became.

"Does your father know about Jeremy?" he asked finally.

"I sent Molly after him. She left about half an hour ago."

"That's good. He'll know what to do." Homan's head began to nod, and a moment later he was sound asleep with his arms outstretched on the table.

Within a few minutes, Anne shook his shoulder. In front of him was a cup of sage tea and a piece of bread and cheese.

"Eat that and go to bed," she said firmly. "I've made up the bed in the loft. You're worn out." She sat down across from him. "But first, I beg you, just a word about Guy," she said. Her eyes had a tender look. "Is he well?"

Homan told her how Guy had helped the people of Newark and of his arrival at night, but he still refrained from mentioning his brother's arrest. "Matt is looking after him," he assured Anne before he climbed to the loft.

He awakened several hours later. Downstairs two men were talking. One was Rufus Warren and the other sounded like Dr. Smith. Homan rolled closer to the open trap door and peered down. Yes, that was the doctor. As he watched, the doctor walked quietly from Jeremy's bed to the kitchen table and sat down opposite Mr. Warren. Anne was beside the bed, putting a wet cloth on her brother's forehead, and Molly was stirring something in a big kettle that hung over the fire.

"It's typhus, without a doubt," the doctor said gravely. "He mustn't be moved. To take him out in such weather would be certain——"

Rufus Warren interrupted him, showing by the tone of his voice that he couldn't bear to have the doctor mention the consequences of moving his son. "We must do what's best for him. Who knows? Perhaps the British won't get this far. I wish I could send my girls to my sister in Batavia, but if I do that, who's to nurse my son? I'd stay, if I weren't sorely needed at Fort Gray."

Anne spoke up. "Let Molly go, Father. I can manage alone."

Molly said indignantly, "I'm not leaving until we all go!"

"Hush!" said her father. He turned to Dr. Smith. "What do you hear of the enemy? Do you think they'll come tonight?"

"I hear only rumors. Some say tonight and some say not at all. As for me, I'm staying here. I have sick people to care for and I'll not leave them."

"Bless you for that," said Rufus.

Molly set a cup of sage tea in front of the doctor. He looked up at her and smiled. "Thank you, Molly. You're getting to be quite a young lady." He sipped the hot drink. Then he asked, "What does young Homan Reed say, Rufus? Why do you ask me what's going to happen when you have our best source of information right in your house?"

"I didn't want to disturb him," Mr. Warren replied. "Anne says he was fair exhausted."

Homan called down, "I'm awake now, sir. I'll be right there." Carrying his shoes, he climbed down the ladder that was built against the wall. He dropped onto a bench beside the table. "General McClure says the British are sure to seek revenge for Newark," he told the men as he pulled on his shoes. "If we're going to stay here, we'd best be prepared."

"But they'll never get past Fort Niagara!" exclaimed Dr. Smith.

"They don't have to get by it," said Homan. "They can cross the river above the fort."

"That's true enough," Dr. Smith agreed. "And our forces here don't amount to much. Most of the militia went home. Can't blame them. The government doesn't send their pay until months after it's due—if at all. And they don't have decent food or lodging."

"Fort Gray can protect the landing at Lewiston," said Mr. Warren.

"Look how they came across and robbed my cow and chickens," Homan pointed out. "We can't be sure they'll come over at the landing."

"What do you propose, young fellow?" asked the doctor.

Thus questioned, Homan felt a little embarrassed, but he answered firmly, "I think we should be ready to fight. I have a musket, but not much ammunition. We all should be armed. Then we can make a stand wherever we are."

Dr. Smith nodded and turned to Rufus Warren. "He's right, you know."

"There's a good supply of armaments at Benjamin Barton's," said Rufus.

Homan was familiar with the big cellar Mr. Barton had made for a fine new house on the hill overlooking the river. The war had interrupted the building and now the cellar, roofed over, was a government storehouse for weapons and ammunition.

"I'll go to Barton's," said the doctor. "We've been depending too much on the militia and they aren't reliable."

He sighed. "It's a terrible pity that McClure put the torch to Newark. A pity for Newark and for us and our whole nation. I'm sure he acted without orders from Washington, but other countries may not understand that."

"You're thinking of our reputation as a nation," said Rufus, "and I agree with you. We're on the way to becoming a great and powerful nation, and we want the rest of the world to look up to us and trust us. Incidents like Newark don't help our cause."

The doctor took another look at Jeremy before he left. He went away shaking his head. "That's a sick boy. Keep him warm and give him the medicine regularly."

After the doctor had gone, Mr. Warren asked, "What are your plans, Homan?"

"To return to Fort Niagara and enlist, sir, as soon as I can."

Mr. Warren leaned his arms on the table and looked him directly in the eyes. "I don't have any right to ask it, but I'm desperate. Will you stay here until Jeremy can be moved? With this threat of attack, I daren't leave Anne and Molly without a man's protection."

Homan was pleased to be called a man and happy to be needed and wanted. His answer would be easy because even before he had gone to sleep in the loft, he had made up his mind that he must stay until Jeremy could be taken to Batavia. It was what Guy would expect of him. Besides, he, himself, cared about the safety of the Warrens.

As he was about to reply, Molly brought steaming bowls of stew to the table. "If you stay, I'll cook for you," she said.

Homan often had eaten Molly's cooking and knew that it was good, but to tease her he pretended to be doubtful.

"Did you make this stew?" he asked.

"Of course."

He lifted a spoonful to his mouth. "It's a terrible chance I'm taking."

Molly turned on her heel and said in her mischievous way, "Take care. It may be poisoned!"

Homan tried to maintain a frown, but the stew was warm and delicious. He smiled and saluted Molly with his spoon. "I'll stay!"

Chapter 10

A Dangerous Game

Homan tiptoed into the cabin with his arms full of firewood. He wiped the snow from his feet, and as quietly as possible, laid the wood in the woodbox.

Molly, preparing porridge for breakfast, nodded her thanks.

Five days had passed since Homan had come to the Warrens'—five days of excitement over the burning of Newark. The entire countryside had been stirred up over the event. A delegation from Lewiston had rowed across the Niagara to offer shelter and food and clothing to the Newark refugees. Brigadier General Peter Porter and other important men from Buffalo and Black Rock had ridden to Fort Niagara to demand an explanation of McClure's action and to plan for the defense of the Niagara frontier. McClure was in disgrace, and on the American side of the river the people daily braced themselves for the expected reprisal on the part of the British.

Inside the Warrens' cabin, the war was often forgotten in concern over Jeremy.

As Homan hung his coat on a peg near the door, he noticed that Anne had fallen asleep in her chair beside her brother's bed. Since his illness, she scarcely stirred from the little boy's side. In the few minutes that she was away, Homan or Molly took her place. But in spite of their care and Dr. Smith's daily visits, Jeremy's fever had stayed high and for two days he had not even recognized anyone.

Homan softly approached the trundle bed and looked down at the sleeping child. The small face seemed less flushed this morning, he thought hopefully. Anne awakened and smiled at Homan. "Good morning," she said softly.

As if he had been waiting for that signal, Jeremy opened his eyes and said clearly, "I'm hungry."

Anne and Homan looked at each other with delight, and Molly came running to find out if she had heard correctly.

From that moment on, Jeremy recovered quickly. Dr. Smith grunted, "Good nursing. If our soldiers got the care you three gave this fellow, we'd have a bigger army. Do you know we lose far more soldiers from disease than from enemy bullets?"

Eight days after the burning of Newark, people began to say the British had decided not to seek revenge. Probably they were afraid to come over and attack. A few warned that the danger was not past.

Rufus Warren had come home almost every evening to see how his son was progressing. When he saw that Jeremy was able to sit up in bed and eat, he said, "We'll pack the sled tonight and be ready for an early start tomorrow."

Anne looked at Jeremy with worried eyes. "He's still so

weak. I'm afraid he'll take a chill. Give him just a little longer. Even if the British come, we've the militia to protect us."

"Well—one more day, then," Rufus said reluctantly. "Gather up our goods and start packing the sled tomorrow. I'll come back as soon as I can to help you." He took his coat from the peg by the door. "I'll be on my way. Before I go up the mountain, I want to pay a visit to my friend, Lothrop. I hear he had to have his leg amputated and he must be in need of cheer."

"May I go, too?" Homan asked. He had always admired Lothrop Cooke, and he remembered well how bravely the man had piloted the boats across the Niagara during the battle for Queenstown Heights. His leg had failed to heal after the injury he had received at that time.

"Get your coat," said Rufus. "I'll be glad of your company."

Homan had an afterthought. "Maybe I should stay—in case of attack."

Anne spoke up quickly. "We'll be all right. You can't stay with us every moment. Leave Shorty to protect us."

The Cooke home was on the Ridge Road a mile east of Lewiston. As Homan and Mr. Warren walked up the road in the failing light, Rufus said, "They were early settlers here— the Cookes. Lemuel, that's Lothrop's father, came to Fort Niagara from Connecticut in 1796. He was with the first American forces to occupy Fort Niagara after the Revolution."

They found Lothrop in bed, and fearing to tire him, Homan and Rufus made their visit brief.

Lothrop's brother, Bates, followed them from the bedroom and closed the door behind him. They all went into the front room, where Bates put a fresh log on the fire and pulled up chairs for his visitors.

"Take my advice and send your family to safety," he advised

Rufus. "If it weren't for Lothrop, we'd have gone east before now. He's getting better every day, but we're still afraid to move him."

Rufus took out his pipe and reached for his tobacco. "When I see a fine big man like your brother in such a sad state, I wonder if anything is worth so great a cost."

"Lothrop has no doubts, nor have I," Bates answered. "This new country of ours is worth fighting for."

"I agree to that," Rufus said heartily. "But is this fight necessary? Think, Bates, only three days after we declared war, Britain repealed her Orders in Council, and thus opened the way for us to trade with France again. Why didn't we make peace then?"

"Britain still would have boarded our ships and impressed our seamen, and she would have continued to arouse the western Indians against our settlers." Bates held a burning taper for Rufus' pipe. "No, we had to fight to show Britain and France, too, that we're a proud nation—one to be treated with respect."

Rufus puffed at his pipe until he had it drawing well. "I daresay you're right. Old John Bull never did treat us right, even after we won our independence fair and square." He stretched his feet out to the warmth of the fire. "I believe the tide of this war will change soon in our favor. Britain had a head start with her supply of experienced officers, but we're developing some good ones of our own."

"Like Commodore Oliver Perry," Homan said eagerly. "He showed his worth in that battle on Lake Erie."

"Right you are," Bates agreed. "Now, if Napoleon Bonaparte will just continue to keep Britain occupied——"

Darkness had fallen by the time Homan and Rufus returned to Lewiston. When they reached the road that climbed the escarpment, Rufus stopped and rested his hand on Homan's shoulder. "I'm thankful you're looking after my family," he said. "May God protect you."

Rufus' sturdy figure disappeared into the darkness, but Homan still felt cheered by the man's trust in him. He knew his size was a matter of indifference to Rufus Warren.

Behind Homan lights shone in the windows of Hustler's Tavern, and as he headed down the street, the front door crashed open. He turned around just in time to see a heavy-set man stagger out. In the light that streamed from the door, he recognized Zeb Humel.

If it had been anyone else from the fort, Homan would have asked him for news of Guy. Since leaving Fort Niagara, he had had no word of his brother's fate. But not for anything would he approach Zeb.

Homan shrank back into the shadow of a tree, glad that Shorty had stayed in the cabin this night. Looking as if he would fall at any moment, Zeb lurched down the steps and swayed along the road past Homan. The door of the tavern slammed shut and Zeb seemed transformed by the sound. He straightened his back and strode off with a walk as steady as a parson's.

That was strange, Homan thought. Why would Zeb pretend to be drunk? It was more than curiosity that made Homan follow him even after they had passed the Warren cabin. Who knew what mischief such a man might do, especially in war time?

Homan kept well behind and stayed in the shadows as much as possible as they passed darkened cabins whose owners had fled east days ago and other homes where firelight and candlelight flickered in the windows.

At Millar's Store a light shone onto the road, so he circled behind the building. When he ventured out again, Zeb had disappeared. Homan paused, wondering which way the man had gone. Straight ahead was the river. Several soldiers were on the docks and two men stood just outside the Porter, Barton and Company storehouse, but the road that sloped down to the docks was empty. To his right was the route to Fort Niagara. At first he thought it, too, was empty, but a hundred feet away, on the left-hand side of the road, a shadowy form moved.

Homan ran lightly across and entered the woods. Here the snow had an icy crust that broke noisily under his feet. Afraid Zeb would hear him, he returned to the edge of the road where he could move more quietly.

As he hurried along, he kept alert to any movement or sound, but Zeb seemed to have vanished. Homan looked anxiously over his shoulder. Had he passed the man? He knew he was playing a dangerous game, for Zeb surely would have no mercy if he caught Homan following him.

Suddenly, just ahead, a horse whinnied, and then with a pounding of hoofs, came out of the woods to the left of the road and galloped away toward Fort Niagara. On the horse's back was Zeb.

He must have had his horse hidden among the trees. Why would he do that? Why not ride up to the door of Hustler's Tavern and tie his horse to the hitching post? A man must have reasons for such unusual actions. A terrible suspicion formed in Homan's mind. Was it possible that Zeb was a British spy? If so, Homan thought, I should have killed him as he paddled across to Canada the night that Newark was burned.

Still puzzling, Homan turned back to Lewiston. As he approached Millar's Store, the light went out and young Alex

Millar emerged, locking the door behind him. Homan had not seen him since that snowy day he had met him on the road to Fort Niagara, when Alex had been on sentry duty.

Homan called out to him, "You're working late, Alex!"

Alex held out his hand. "You're wandering abroad late, yourself."

They stood together in the shelter of the doorway. "I've been following a villain," Homan said with a grin. "Do you know Zeb Humel?"

"No."

"Then you're fortunate." He told Alex of his encounters with Zeb. "Strange actions, aren't they?" he concluded.

Alex said excitedly, "Strange, indeed! He might be a spy!"

"I'm beginning to think so, too."

Alex went on. "And you say he's a gunsmith, favored by the officers at the fort. Think of the secrets he can overhear and pass on to the British." He clapped his mittened hand to his thigh. "You must report this to Major Bennett!"

Homan said hesitantly, "It's a terrible thing to call someone a spy. Suppose I'm wrong?"

"Suppose you're right and you don't report him! He may be the death of all of us!"

"I guess you're right," Homan said slowly.

"Come! I'll go with you to headquarters. I'm going there, anyway, to find out what hours I'm on watch."

As they left the doorway, Homan pulled his cap over his ears. "I don't envy you a watch by the river tonight."

"I can't say I'm looking forward to it, but I have no choice. We're short of men. Some have been on duty every night for over a week."

Homan felt ashamed of himself. He had been so busy at the

Warrens' that he hadn't even thought of volunteering for the river patrol. Well, he had done what he had to do. "The British are slow about their revenge," he said.

"True. Tomorrow's December nineteenth. Nine days since Newark burned."

"Perhaps they won't come at all."

"We daren't take a chance on that. I think they'll come, and so does Major Bennett. By the way, have you heard the signal he's arranged with Captain Leonard?"

"No."

"The cannon at Fort Niagara is to be fired three times if the fort is attacked," said Alex. "One or two shots would be a false alarm. So if you hear three, hurry the Warrens to safety."

"I'm taking them to Batavia day after tomorrow," Homan told him. "Jeremy's fever has broken."

"Glad to hear that," Alex said heartily. "We talk of going, but we have livestock to feed, so we stay on."

They had reached the building used as headquarters by the commander of the militia. Alex rapped on the door and a weary-looking young soldier admitted the two boys to a shadowy room, lighted only by a lamp set on a bare, wooden table. "You can't see Major Bennett tonight," he told them when they asked. "He's in an important conference and can't be disturbed."

Alex searched out the time of his patrol on a paper that lay beside the lamp, and Homan followed him outside without saying a word about Zeb Humel. Morning would be soon enough to speak to the Major. Surely he couldn't tell that sleepy young volunteer of his suspicion of Zeb.

A light snow had begun to fall, and flakes tickled Homan's face as he ran down the street to the Warrens' place.

A homey scene met his eyes as he opened the door. Anne

was setting the table for the next day's breakfast and Molly, beside the fire, was knitting a long scarf of a deep blue color. Anne turned to him with a welcoming smile, and Shorty ran to him with his tail wagging like a whip.

Molly said tartly, "We thought you'd been kidnaped—like Belinda."

"Better than that," said Homan. "I was following a spy!"

Molly looked up, her eyes bright with interest, but then she ducked her head over her knitting and said. "A likely story."

But when she heard Homan's account of Zeb Humel, she was inclined to agree that he might, indeed, be a spy.

Chapter 11

Flight from Death

It was still dark when Homan was awakened by a loud noise. The echo of a dull boom still rang in his ears. The cannons at Fort Niagara! He got up and shouted below, "Wake up! I just heard the cannons at the fort!"

Shorty jumped up from the rug by the fire and barked excitedly.

Homan flung on his clothes. Alex Millar had said the signal would be three shots. He had heard only one. That might mean a false alarm. On the other hand, perhaps he had slept through the first two. Just to be sure, they would pack the sled and be on their way. He knew that's what Mr. Warren would want. He dropped his bedding through the trap door and heard it land with a thud on the floor below.

Molly poked her head around the edge of the curtain that sheltered her bed. "What are you doing?" she demanded. "We're not leaving until tomorrow."

"That shot just changed our plans," Homan announced.

Molly grumbled, "Anyone would think that was the first cannon you ever heard."

"It's a signal," said Homan. Hastily he repeated what Alex had told him.

"Molly, get dressed," Anne said sharply. "Papa left Homan in charge, and I agree with him that we'd better get ready to leave."

Outside, Homan brushed last night's snow from the sled, and then hurried to get the oxen. He wondered what was happening at Fort Niagara and hoped that Guy was safe. His heart leaped at the sound of hoofbeats approaching. Were the British here already?

It was Alex Millar's brother who appeared on a lathered horse. Shouting, "The Indians are coming!" he sped on.

Homan raced to the cabin door. Even before he reached it, he heard in the distance a howling yell that filled him with terror. This was no false alarm! Shorty whimpered and dived under the sled.

Opening the door, Homan cried, "Indians! They're coming!" Then he raced back to hitch up the oxen. Stumbling with haste, he returned to the cabin and snatched Jeremy from his bed. He threw a blanket around him and ran out again. Anne and Molly came close after, their arms full of blankets.

Again Homan heard the shrieks of the Indians, this time closer. Molly gasped, and Jeremy began to cry.

Anne took her brother and climbed onto the back of the

sled. Molly leaped in beside them, and Homan started the oxen, running beside them and urging them on. Shorty darted this way and that, as if bewildered.

As they turned onto the road, a wagon drawn by a team of horses flashed past. It rocked back and forth, and the people in it clung to its sides. They kept their eyes on the road ahead of them as if they dared not look back.

The oxen moved with agonizing slowness, and Homan thought they would have a better chance of escape on foot, but he knew they could not run far, carrying Jeremy.

A flurry of shots sounded behind them and a woman's scream was cut off with terrible abruptness.

As Homan prodded the oxen, the road began to fill with frightened people in wagons, sleighs, on horseback, or on foot.

Cattle, sheep, and pigs, driven by their owners, slowed the human traffic. Shorty soon disappeared into the crowd. Homan hoped he was safe, but had no time to look for him.

A woman carrying a baby burst out of a cabin to the right of the road and ran distractedly toward the Warrens' sled.

"Jump aboard!" Homan called.

She shook her head. "I can't find my Johnny! I sent him out to milk the cow and now he's gone. Will you take the baby?"

Molly held out her arms, and the woman thrust the baby into them. Then she ran back toward her cabin.

"We're going to Batavia!" Molly shouted after her. "To my Aunt Patience!"

"Patience Comstock!" Anne added.

The woman didn't pause, and Homan wondered if she had heard them.

"Get on there!" he shouted to the oxen. "Or you'll have arrows in your backsides!"

An exclamation from Anne made him look back over his shoulder just in time to see a man fall slowly from his horse onto the road in front of Millar's Store. An Indian with a tomahawk raised over his head ran toward him.

Molly lifted her head, but Homan said tensely, "Don't look."

"You're right," she answered softly and leaned over the baby.

Homan felt suffocated with helpless anger. So this was the British revenge for the burning of Newark! The Americans had spared the lives of all the inhabitants there, but here the Indians were killing people. Where were the British, anyway? So far he had seen and heard only their Indian allies.

The oxen plodded on, while the whoops of the Indians and the cries of their victims sounded ever nearer.

Every moment Homan expected to feel an arrow or a musket ball in his back or to see an Indian bearing down on them brandishing a tomahawk. He lost all hope when the members of the militia who had been stationed at Lewiston to protect the village came down the road as fast as they could go, having abandoned their cannons.

At last the oxen got the sled outside of the town, and then Anne said, "They're burning everything." Flames shot into the air and smoke billowed high.

When they were a mile beyond the town, Homan saw a team of oxen hitched to a sled in front of the home of the Cooke family. The sled was thickly covered with straw, and as they approached, they saw Bates Cooke and his father run out of the house with blankets and spread them over the straw. A moment later, Bates rushed back inside and came out carrying Lothrop in his arms. Gently he laid him in the sled. The boys' father dashed out of the house, carrying a large brass kettle that he hung over a stake at the rear of the sled. Then he, too, jumped aboard.

People save the strangest things, Homan thought. Of all the furnishings in his house, Mr. Cooke had brought out that kettle. And Molly had saved her knitting; he had glimpsed the blue scarf among the blankets.

Just as he maneuvered the oxen past the Cooke sled, he heard footsteps thudding up the road behind him. He turned quickly and was relieved to see that it was Willard Smith, Jeremy's doctor. He had a musket in his hand and was breathless from running.

Stopping beside the Cookes's sled, he panted, "Bates, is your gun loaded?"

"No," answered Bates. "I have no cartridges."

"Well, I have two." Dr. Smith held out his hand to Bates.

"Load your gun with one and I'll load mine with the other."

Bates shouted his thanks and the Cookes's team started forward slowly under his careful guidance.

Homan groaned. "I forgot my musket!" He looked back toward Lewiston where the billowing smoke told him how useless it would be to try to return for the gun. He remembered running out of the cabin with Jeremy in his arms. He had been in such a hurry that he had left the musket behind. At any moment the Mohawks might catch up with them and he had no weapon at all.

Dr. Smith, still breathing heavily, trotted up beside Homan.

"Jump on the sled, sir," Homan suggested, "and catch your breath."

"Thank you," said the doctor. He leaped on beside Anne. "How's my patient?" he asked.

Jeremy looked up, bright-eyed, from the blankets that enfolded him. "I'm fine! Only I wish I could get out and fight those Indians."

Dr. Smith patted the boy's head. "By the time you're old enough to carry a gun, I hope wars will be over." He lay back on the floor of the sled, drawing deep breaths. In a few minutes, he jumped back to the ground and joined Homan beside the team.

"I hear Fort Niagara has fallen," he said quietly, for Homan's ears alone. "The cannon shot was a signal for a separate force of British and Indians to attack Lewiston. It was a complete surprise to us. You saw our militia. They were among the first to leave."

Homan was dismayed by the word that the fort had fallen. "How could they take the fort so quickly?" he asked.

"Perhaps it's only a rumor," said the doctor. "But the woman who told me heard it from a British officer. He was quite a gentleman, she said. He came down the street just as she and her little boy were fleeing their house, and he saw her safely to the edge of the village. Told her the British don't kill helpless women and children." Dr. Smith waved his hand to the Warrens. "I'll be going on," he said. "Thank you for letting me ride."

If Fort Niagara had fallen, what had become of Guy? Homan wondered.

The oxen continued their slow, steady pace. Homan could see the white steam of their breath. His gaze took in the people on the road before him. Look at all of us, he said to himself. We've known for days that the British might come, and yet we did nothing about it. Last night Bates told us to go to a safer place, but he didn't even get cartridges for his gun—and Dr. Smith had only two. I guess we didn't believe it really would happen.

Homan and the Warrens had almost reached the hollow where the road to the Tuscarora Reservation turned off when they heard close behind them the wild shrieks of the Mohawks. Homan looked back and saw five Indians on horseback closing in on the Cooke sled, which was not far behind. The Indian in the lead had a sword in his hand. He galloped close to the sled and swung at the sick man who lay there.

Homan watched with horror, but just as the Indian brought his sword down, the brass kettle on the back of the sled rattled. His horse shied back at the sound and the sword struck harmlessly at the air. The Indian quickly recovered and again rode forward, but this time Bates was ready. Homan saw him lift his musket. At the same moment, the Mohawks coming up from the rear sent out a volley of shots.

Molly quickly laid the baby on the bottom of the sled and leaned protectively over it. Homan was not surprised. Somehow he had always known there was courage underneath Molly's mischief.

The shots missed the men in the sled behind them, and Bates had made good use of his one cartridge and had brought down the Indian who had swung at his brother. Still, four Mohawks were in close pursuit, and Bates had no more ammunition. This is it, thought Homan. He looked frantically around for shelter, wondering if they should try to run into the woods of the Reservation to the right of the road.

To his surprise, he saw someone in the woods, gliding from one tree to another. The familiar voice of Dave Cusick hailed him.

"Dave!" shouted Homan. "Help us!"

Dave whirled and ran out of sight. Seconds later, from the woods and from the escarpment above, came the sound of gunfire and a wild war whoop.

The Mohawks pursuing the Cooke sled paused, then came forward more slowly. The din on the hillside continued. Horns blew, guns were fired, and war whoops came from many throats.

The Tuscaroras! Homan almost collapsed with relief. Dave and all the friendly Tuscaroras had come to their rescue!

Now the Mohawks stopped completely as bullets whizzed toward them. They fired one more volley, then wheeled and fled back the way they had come.

During the exchange of gunfire Homan heard a soft cry from the rear of the sled, but when he had time to look he could see nothing amiss with his four passengers. Molly was sitting cross-legged, rocking the baby in her arms, and Anne was near the tail of the sled bent over Jeremy.

A shout came from the trees to the right of the road. Out came a Tuscarora chief, little Colonel Jacobs, followed by a small group of braves. One of them was Dave, who ran up to Homan.

"We scare them good," he said with a grin.

Homan looked at the few Indians and asked, "How did you make all that noise? I thought you had an army. And so did those Mohawks!"

Dave pointed toward the escarpment. "Women and children. Everyone in Tuscarora village come out and blow horns and march with guns and sticks and make Mohawk think we have big army."

"You saved our lives," said Homan. "We'd all be dead if you and the other Tuscaroras hadn't stopped the Mohawks."

Dave said calmly, "You my friend." He nodded down the road toward Lewiston. "We not safe yet. More come." He hurried on, calling to a group of his friends who were running down the hill toward the road.

Homan saw that Dave was right. Smoke arose from a cabin he had passed only a few minutes before. He urged the oxen forward.

Colonel Jacobs ran along beside Homan. Next to him, Homan felt tall, yet he knew this man had great spirit.

"At Four Corners is cabin with many guns," said Jacobs. "Tuscarora stop there and make a stand."

Homan knew the place he meant. At the next crossroads was a log cabin where a small arsenal had been set up. "I'll stay, too," he offered.

"Good," said the Indian. "We need many men." He called to four men who were hurrying up the road on foot. "You stop at cabin up ahead and fight Mohawk?"

One of the men answered, "I say we should stop just long enough to blow up the arsenal so the British can't use it."

"No," replied Colonel Jacobs. "We make a stand to give women and children time to get away."

Three of the men shook their heads and trotted on, but the fourth said, "You're right. I'll see you there."

Molly looked scornfully at the backs of the three men who had refused to fight. She crawled to the front of the sled. "I'm staying with you, Homan. If we don't stand together, the Mohawks will kill us all one at a time."

"What about that baby?" asked Homan. "You must go on with Anne and Jeremy. This is a job for men."

"Pa taught me to shoot, so what difference does it make if I'm a girl?" Molly called back to her sister. "You can manage without me, can't you?"

Anne was still leaning over Jeremy, but slowly she turned. Now Homan could see that she was clutching her left shoulder and that a stain was spreading down the sleeve of her brown coat.

"I'm hit," she said in a whisper.

Molly crawled back to Anne.

Homan was filled with anguish, but he stayed with the oxen and left the inspection to Molly. She had more knowledge of such matters than he, for she had helped care for the wounded after the battle of Queenstown Heights. He felt he had failed Mr. Warren and Guy. In some way, he should have protected Anne. Perhaps if he had remembered his gun, he could have saved her. Now he could only keep the oxen going as fast as possible and pray that Anne's injury was not serious.

Molly called to him, "It's a bad wound, Homan. I'm trying to stop the bleeding, but she needs a doctor. Don't leave us, will you?"

"Of course not," he answered indignantly.

They were now at the log cabin arsenal, where Colonel Jacobs was passing out muskets to the few men who had gathered there.

Homan longed to stop. He felt ashamed to go on with the women and children. Dave saw him and shouted, "Homan! You said you'd fight!"

Homan pointed to the rear of the sled. "Anne's badly hurt. I have to go on!"

Dave nodded, and Homan knew he understood. War! he thought. How had he ever believed it would be glorious? War was losing everything you'd worked for, and it was innocent people like Anne getting shot.

Hoofs thundered on the road behind him and war whoops burst from Mohawk throats. Bullets sang through the air. Looking back over his shoulder, Homan saw Dave, little Colonel Jacobs, and the other men taking positions behind trees and in the shelter of the building. They were so few. Could they hold back the Mohawks?

Then Dave ran up the road after the Warrens' sled. "Here, Homan! Gun for you!" He thrust a musket and some ammunition into his friend's hands and darted back again.

Homan loaded the musket and laid it on the sled. If the Mohawks broke through, he now had a chance to save the lives of those in his care.

Chapter 12

Hardscrabble Camp

One month later, Homan and Shorty threaded their way down the crowded main street of Batavia. Refugees from Lewiston and Youngstown, from Black Rock, Buffalo, and Manchester jostled each other or loitered on the fringe of the crowd. Many had lost their homes and all they possessed when the British and their Indian allies had laid waste the frontier along the Niagara River all the way from Fort Niagara south to Buffalo. Like Youngstown and Lewiston, the towns of Manchester, Schlosser, Black Rock, and Buffalo were now only ashes.

A bulletin board outside the offices of the Holland Land Company drew Homan's attention. A group had gathered there to read an announcement. He joined them and read:

HELP ASKED FOR VICTIMS OF THE BURNING

There followed a list of the sufferers. His own name was on the paper, along with those of young Alex Millar, who was now a prisoner in Canada, and Dr. Smith, whose home and office had been burned.

"I hear the legislature in Albany voted money to help," one man remarked.

"The city of Albany has sent one thousand dollars," said another.

"New York City is giving three thousand dollars."

"All that distance away and they send money to us!"

"That's the way it is in a democracy, my friend!"

Homan turned away from the lists of names and losses. He wanted no money, though he was sure the cabin he and Guy had shared was gone. Right now he wanted to find out what had happened to his brother and to help to drive out the enemy. They still held Fort Niagara and controlled most of the land along the Niagara River, and until they were gone, none of the refugees could go home.

Another item on the bulletin board drew him:

MEN! ENLIST TO SAVE YOUR COUNTRY! SIGN UP TODAY!

This notice was signed by Major General Amos Hall.

Homan had heard this morning that Hall was collecting an army and he had determined to enlist. This time nothing could stop him. Anne was recovering nicely from her bullet wound and Jeremy was strong again. Their father was now stationed in the ruined village of Buffalo. He and the rest of the little garrison under Major Mallory at Fort Gray had fought gallantly. When the British had pushed them from the fort, they had retreated slowly, giving the people of Manchester a chance to escape.

The baby Molly had cared for on that cold and frightening journey from Lewiston was now back with its mother, and Molly was busy helping her Aunt Patience cook for the suddenly increased household. But busy as she was, she had found time to finish the blue scarf which Homan now wore.

A group of men and teen-aged boys was gathered outside the Major General's headquarters. They were new recruits and they were eagerly discussing their future.

"I hear we're going to Hardscrabble. Hall is sending a big force there."

"Hardscrabble? Where's that?"

"On the Ridge, about six miles this side of Lewiston. Used to be a little settlement, just a few log cabins. There's a camp there now—nearest we have to the Niagara."

Hardscrabble. It had a lonely, rough sound, but Homan didn't care. He was ready for danger—anything rather than the inaction of the past month. He had had enough to do— odd jobs to bring in money to feed himself and the Warrens. Besides, he had done the endless wood-splitting, fire-tending, and water-carrying necessary to keep the household fed and warm. But he was restless, for none of these tasks was helping him to find Guy and none could bring this war any nearer to its close.

Still followed by Shorty, Homan pushed through the group of recruits. On entering the building, he found himself in a crowded room where several officers sat behind a narrow table.

This time he heard no remarks about his size. The officer in charge handed him a pen and said, "Sign here," pointing to the muster roll, which already covered several pages.

One of the onlookers laughed and said, "Let the dog sign up, too."

Homan felt six inches taller as he walked out of the building. At last he was a member of the army, and he, too, was headed for the camp in the wilderness—Hardscrabble. Perhaps there he could find out more about Guy. Though he had questioned many soldiers during the past month, and Rufus Warren had helped him draft an official inquiry to the War Department, he still didn't know what had become of his brother. He had been at Fort Niagara, that was certain, but he was not listed as a prisoner of the British and his name was not on the roll of those killed.

General Hall assigned Lieutenant Colonel Harris to accompany the recruits to Hardscrabble Camp—a march of a little over forty miles. The men started out cheerfully, singing to set the pace and to keep up their spirits. But as the miles unfolded behind them, they became silent.

The soldier next to Homan remarked with bravado, "Wouldn't want the noise to scare those Britishers."

Looking about at the faces around him, Homan knew it wasn't the British who would be most afraid. He felt the uneasiness growing the farther behind they left the friendly town of Batavia. The wilderness crowded close to the narrow, uneven road, and who knew how many Mohawks might be hiding in those dim woods?

At night they slept on the ground, with fires to keep away wild animals and sentinels to watch for human enemies.

Many of the marching men were still haunted by the memory of their flight up this very road only a little more than a month ago. The Tuscaroras and a handful of settlers had stopped the Mohawks at the arsenal at Four Corners, but those who continued down the road had not felt safe for miles past that. In fact, for days, Batavia and other towns to the east had prepared for attack. But instead of continuing to move to the east, the British had followed the Niagara south. Even the thriving little harbor town of Buffalo was burned to the ground, except for one house owned by the Widow St. John, a blacksmith shop, and the stone jail.

Late on the third day of marching, Hardscrabble Camp came into view. Homan was disappointed to see the few log buildings. It surely didn't look like a fortress in the wilderness. There were not enough barracks for all the men, and he was assigned to a tent. He flung his blanket roll onto the cot with its lumpy straw mattress and went outside with several of the men, planning to take a tour of inspection around the camp before dark.

A soldier came down the path carrying two huge iron kettles, one of which he deposited in front of Homan.

"Hope you fellows know how to cook," he said. "I pity you if you can't."

"Y'mean we fix our own victuals?" demanded one of the new recruits.

"You do if you want to eat," the kettle-bearer replied. "Only the top officers have a cook. I hear he's a good one, too. Used to cook at Hustler's Tavern."

Homan's ears pricked up at this, and after a meal that was only tolerable, he searched out the officers' kitchen. There, as he had hoped, was Matt Pomeroy, eating his dinner at a well-scrubbed table.

Matt dropped his spoon. "Homan!" He leaped up, almost overturning the table in his haste to pound Homan on the back, for all the world as if he were a long-lost relative.

After their first happy greetings, Homan asked, "Do you have any word of Guy?"

Matt put a wedge of johnnycake before Homan and sat down opposite him. "I daresay you're still hungry," he growled. "We're short of provisions, as usual." He poured a mug of tea. "I've had no word of your brother since the British took Fort Niagara, but of that last day I can tell you much."

So while Homan munched on the johnnycake and soaked in the warmth of the kitchen fire, Matt told him of the attack on Fort Niagara.

"The British came at about three or four in the morning on December nineteenth," he said, "the same day they burned Youngstown and Lewiston. They had the password—got it from the guard at Campbell's Tavern in Youngstown—and then killed every one of the forty men in the tavern."

Homan recalled the lonely sentry he had met outside Campbell's Tavern, waiting for a card player from inside to replace him.

"They had no trouble getting inside the fort," Matt went on. "They were quiet, and the gate wasn't even locked. Besides, they brought scaling ladders with them, and before we knew what was going on, they were over the stockade and had us at their mercy. By dawn there were Irish soldiers dancing a jig on the gun deck of the Mess House. I heard 'em myself from the woods where I was hiding. I even recognized the tune —'St. Patrick's Day,' it was."

"But what about Guy?" asked Homan impatiently. He knew well enough that the fort had fallen and that all of the supplies stored there were in British hands. "Last I knew he was headed for jail."

"He didn't spend an hour in jail, thanks to me," said Matt with a proud smile. "I convinced Captain Leonard he didn't belong there. McClure sputtered, but he gave in. He had bigger problems to worry about. I said I'd be responsible for Guy and that I needed him in the kitchen, so that's where he came. He was good help, too. Well, the night of the attack, he headed straight for the Red Barracks where all the hospital patients were. We had a parcel of them. A hundred were from the battle at Detroit. With my own eyes I saw Guy standing at the door to the hospital holding off half a dozen attackers. Last I saw of him, he went down there in the doorway."

Tears came to Homan's eyes. "Did they kill him?"

"I can't say. I tried to get to him, but I had a battle of my own right then, and I never laid eyes on him again. After a while, I saw my chance to escape. I dived over a place where the stockade was broken down and made haste to get to the woods. Not many of us reached safety that day."

"Do you think there's any hope that Guy escaped?"

"I don't know. I wish I could tell you."

"He isn't listed as a prisoner or as being killed," said Homan, unable to give up hope.

"Perhaps he's a prisoner and his name failed to get on the list," Matt suggested, but Homan feared that his friend said this only to comfort him.

He struggled to keep his voice steady. "I never thought Fort Niagara could be taken. How did the gate happen to be open?"

"There were many strange happenings that night," Matt said. He shoved his empty dishes to one side and a kitchen helper took them away to be washed. "Captain Leonard was in command of the fort, as you know, but he wasn't even there when the British arrived. He went home that night about eleven, leaving orders that he be called if there were signs of an attack. Some say his wife is expecting their first child and he was worried about her. Be that as it may, there never was time to go after him. I saw him gallop up to the fort after it was all over. Guess he surrendered himself to the British." Matt scratched his head. "He had posted guards aplenty to watch for trouble. One at least should have seen the enemy coming. Myself, I suspect treachery. Treason in our own ranks."

Matt's words brought back to Homan the memory of a squat figure hurrying across a dark, snowy road.

"The night I left Fort Niagara, I saw Zeb Humel cross the river in a canoe—my own canoe, by the way. And the night before the British attacked, he came out of Hustler's Tavern for all the world as if he was drunk, but as soon as the door closed behind him, he walked sober and straight."

Matt looked up, and his eyes gleamed in the firelight. "Zeb Humel? The chap who knocked you down outside the fort?"

Homan nodded.

"He's here at Hardscrabble," Matt said grimly. "I saw him this very afternoon."

Chapter 13

ͰͰͰͰͰͰͰͰͰͰͰͰͰ

In Enemy Territory

Zeb Humel at Hardscrabble! Homan glanced back over his shoulder, half-expecting to discover the man's ugly face peering from the shadows. He saw only the kitchen workers, intent on cleaning the pots in which the evening meal had been cooked. Had any of them been near enough to overhear his remarks about Zeb?

He stood up. "Let's go outside. I need a breath of air."

Matt looked surprised, but he followed him without a question. A lantern hanging beside the door threw a faint yellow light onto the snow. Matt shivered in his shirt sleeves. "Make it short."

Homan leaned close. "I'm going to talk to Colonel Harris about Zeb. Where'll I find him?"

Matt pointed to the left. "There. See through those trees."

Homan saw a faint light in the distance. He guessed it came from a window.

"Careful, though," warned Matt. "Don't tell anyone but Harris or Colonel Swift. I pity you if Zeb ever gets wind of what you're suggesting! Maybe you'd better think it over."

"No!" Homan exclaimed, louder than he had intended. He lowered his voice. "I waited before, and the next morning the British attacked Fort Niagara and burned Lewiston and Youngstown. Perhaps if I hadn't waited, our homes would be standing today."

Matt whispered back, "D'you think Zeb had something to do with the British attack?"

"I don't know. But he was on some errand that night. He may have told the British the way was clear for attack. Or arranged that the gate would be open at the fort." He shook his head. "This time I daren't wait."

"I'll get you a lantern." Matt started toward the door.

Homan caught his arm. "No! I can find my way. I'll be safer if no one sees me."

"You need a light," Matt insisted. "Every man here is nervous and thinks any shadow that moves is an Indian. You'd likely get a bullet in your skull if you went prowling over there in the dark."

As Homan followed the narrow path through the trees, walking with a lantern, he wished he had the company of Shorty. The dog was better off in Batavia, though. This rough army camp in the midst of the wilderness was no place for him. He smiled grimly to himself. It was no place for a human being, either.

A gust of wind shook the limbs of the trees and sent a fine, powdery snow onto Homan's cap and down his neck. No wonder the people who originally settled this place had called it Hardscrabble. They must have had to struggle fiercely to make a living here. He wondered where they were now. It seemed to him a strange place to build a village, even though there was a good spring and it was near the Ridge Road. But it was not on a waterway, which was where towns usually started.

Lieutenant Colonel Harris listened to Homan's account of Zeb's strange actions, and then he excused himself to discuss the matter with Colonel Swift. When he returned, he said gravely, "Thank you for coming to me, young man, but Colonel Swift knows Zeb Humel well, and he assures me that his loyalty is above reproach. He wants your word that you'll say nothing further about this to anyone."

Homan was so astonished that he dared to protest. "But why would he paddle over to Canada?"

"It was dark, you said. Mayhap it was someone else you saw."

"It was Zeb," Homan said positively. "And, pardon me, sir, there was that night he pretended to be drunk."

"A joke," suggested Harris. "He was playing the fool for some friends."

Unconvinced, Homan took his leave and made his way back to Matt to report on his unsuccessful mission.

"No doubt Colonel Swift knows more about Zeb than you do," Matt said. "But even colonels can be wrong. We'll keep open minds."

"Colonel Swift didn't see Zeb cross to Canada as I did," Homan replied. "I *know* it was Zeb who took my canoe. And that night when he left Hustler's, he wasn't playing a game. He was in dead earnest and he was in a hurry."

That night Homan lay awake for hours, tormented by the

cold and the snoring of his companions. When he slept, it was to dream of Zeb leading the enemy to Hardscrabble Camp.

Daylight found him as distrustful of Zeb as ever and uneasy at the prospect of meeting him. No wonder the British had been able to take the whole Niagara Frontier, he thought, if all the American commanders were so indifferent to spies. What kind of proof did they need before they'd realize Zeb was a dangerous man to have around?

That morning Zeb passed within a few feet of the campfire over which Homan was cooking breakfast. Fear made the back of his neck prickle as the man's narrow eyes met his. A curt nod was his only greeting.

Shortly after breakfast, a bugle call brought everyone to the parade ground. Colonel Harris strode onto the field and lifted his hand for their attention. Homan, waiting among the uneven ranks, listened intently. Harris had to shout to be heard above the rumble of talk among the soldiers.

Patrols were to be sent to Lewiston, Manchester, and Fort Schlosser, he said. Their mission would be to find out if the enemy was stationed at or near the site of these settlements, which of course, were now in ashes. "We want to know," said Colonel Harris, "to what extent the British are occupying the land along the Niagara. Are they setting up big camps all along it or are they staying close to the fort? The patrols should go as near as possible to the enemy and return with all the information they can collect."

The ranks were quiet now.

"Private Zeb Humel will be in charge of the patrol to Schlosser and Manchester," Lieutenant Colonel Harris announced.

Homan was stunned. Zeb was a strange choice for leader. He might well turn the whole patrol over to the British! Homan wanted to shout his protest, but Harris had made him promise he would say nothing futher about his suspicion of Zeb.

The voice of Colonel Harris broke through his thoughts. "I want volunteers for the patrol to Schlosser and Manchester."

A murmur ran through the ranks and then several of the men stepped forward. Homan glanced at the volunteers. Some, he knew, loved excitement and danger. Others had a sincere desire to help their country, and still others preferred anything to the inactivity of camp life.

Homan drew in a deep breath of the sharp winter air. Although he was tired from the long trip of the past three days and from his restless night, he knew that he, too, must volunteer. Much as he feared Zeb Humel, he would join the patrol to Manchester and Schlosser and never take his eyes from the leader.

Moving to the front, he gave his name in a clear voice, "Homan Reed!" To his left another soldier volunteered. It was Matt Pomeroy.

When the members of the patrol met in the officers' mess hall for instructions, Matt pulled Homan aside. "Why did you volunteer? Are you in a hurry to die?"

"Why did you?" countered Homan.

"To look after you. They'll just have to find someone else to cook for them!"

Homan said angrily, "You'd better quit right now. I don't need a guardian."

"I had another reason, too," Matt confessed. "I want to see what's left of Manchester so I can tell my girl."

"Your girl!" Homan laughed.

Matt nodded and turned red. "Her name's Mary Lou and she used to live in Manchester."

"I have a girl, too," Homan said. It was the first time he had admitted, even to himself, that Molly was his girl. At least she was the one he wanted. He wondered what she'd do if he asked her to be his girl. Probably she'd throw something at me, he thought, though she *had* given him the blue scarf.

Matt did not seem to be surprised at Homan's announcement. "It's Molly Warren, I've no doubt. She's a bonny lass, though a mite too smart for my taste. Good luck to you."

"Thank you. I . . ." Homan broke off as Zeb entered the hall. He glanced toward the man. "There's my reason for volunteering."

Matt nodded. "So I guessed. We'll both watch him."

As the little patrol of twenty-five men rode away from Hardscrabble on horseback, each man was armed with a musket and carried a bayonet point at his side. Each had food enough for the day.

The Ridge Road down which the residents of Lewiston had fled a month before was deeply covered with snow. Not a footprint marred the smooth track between the trees. Homan urged his horse forward until he was near the beginning of the line. Here he could keep Zeb Humel's broad back in sight.

Soon they branched to the left and climbed the escarpment through the Tuscarora Reservation. The little village was a desolate sight, for all of its buildings had been leveled. The British and their Indians had set fire to it to punish the Tuscaroras for helping the American settlers. Only a blackened timber poked above the snow where Dave Cusick's home had been. Even the sawmill, of which the Indians had been so proud, was burned.

The snow on the top of the escarpment was deeper than on the lake plain below. Zeb Humel kept a southwesterly course, through little-known trails where the horses floundered in snow up to their flanks. The sun had passed its zenith when Zeb sent the order down the line for a halt to rest, feed and water the horses, and for the men to eat. Homan had only begun his lunch when Zeb leaped onto his horse and the brief stop was over. Homan munched on jerked beef as he rode along, wondering why the patrol leader was in such a hurry.

Half an hour after their stop, they saw ahead of them a spiral of smoke. Zeb halted and the entire patrol gathered around him.

"It may be an enemy campfire," he warned.

The patrol approached warily, but the smoke turned out to be from the chimney of a small log cabin. The bearded man who came to the door was glad to see the blue uniforms.

"I hear the British and their Indians make raids every now and then on some poor settler like me who came back to his land," he said. "Glad to say I haven't seen any around here yet."

About a mile northeast of Manchester, Zeb again brought the patrol to a halt. "The snow has made us late. Now the only way I can see for us to scout around Manchester and Schlosser and still return to Hardscrabble tonight is to break up into two groups. We don't want to be caught in enemy territory after dark."

Immediately Homan's suspicions came alive. This was a small enough patrol as it was, and to break it up seemed to be courting trouble.

"The larger group will go south to Schlosser, and I'll take two or three good men west with me to Manchester. Both places are about a mile from here." His eyes raked over the men. "Reed, I'll take you with me." He paused, and in the quiet Matt said, "How about me?"

Zeb nodded. "I'll accept your offer, Pomeroy. The rest of you go straight ahead to the Portage Road. Take that south to Schlosser. We'll all leave our horses here. We can be quieter on foot. Now spread out and go from tree to tree the way the Indians do. If you see the enemy, stay out of sight but keep your eyes open. Look for any signs of occupation. We want to know if the British have any men stationed here. As soon as you've looked around, come back here and we'll return to Hardscrabble together."

Three soldiers were left with the horses, and the others proceeded to the south. Homan watched them dart from tree to tree like a family of squirrels.

Zeb motioned to him and Matt to draw close. "I understand the Eagle Tavern and two or three other log buildings are still standing in Manchester. The Colonel wants to know if the British are using them as barracks."

As they entered the little village, they could see in the distance the mist from the falls, rising like an earth-born cloud. But they had no time to admire its beauty. Their eyes were busy, searching for signs of the enemy. Cautiously they advanced down the main street—a narrow road edged by trees, with now and then the rubble of a log house.

Several times they saw footprints in the snow.

"A day or so old," Zeb commented. "But they warrant caution."

Gradually Homan was losing some of his mistrust of Zeb. The patrol leader seemed intent only on doing his job.

They climbed a slight rise and here Homan noticed an unusually large oak.

"From the top of that I could get a far view," he suggested.

Zeb agreed. "A good idea."

"I'll give you a boost," offered Matt.

Homan clutched his musket firmly in one hand, and with Matt's help, scrambled up the tree. As he went higher, he discovered that he had indeed a splendid view of the country-side. From here he could see part of the great waterfall, plunging blue-green over the rim of the precipice. Between him and the falls stood a good-sized building. That must be the Eagle Tavern. He studied it carefully, but saw no signs of life. Leaning this way and that, he surveyed the entire village. Nothing moved on the silent landscape except the mist above the falls.

He looked down, intending to tell Matt that he could not see anyone, but his friend was no longer at the foot of the tree. A moment later, he discovered Matt a short distance away, standing motionless, staring at Zeb Humel. Zeb, with his head thrust forward on his short neck, was examining the ground. Suddenly he leaped up and whirled around with a speed that seemed impossible for so stocky a man.

As if on signal, four British soldiers ran from the cover of the trees with muskets leveled.

Chapter 14

A Spy Is Unmasked

Stunned by the sudden appearance of the redcoats, Homan clung to the tree as if frozen there.

Matt started to load his musket, but two of the British soldiers were upon him before he had time to drop the cartridge into the muzzle. Though he swung wildly with his gun, using it as a club, his attackers dodged skillfully and in seconds had him disarmed. Even in the excitement of the moment, Homan admired the ability of the British. They were well-trained, for a certainty.

In the meantime, Zeb, who had reached for his bayonet, had a British point nudging his chest before he had his bayonet affixed to his musket.

Quietly, Homan settled himself in a crotch of the tree with his back against the trunk. Moving cautiously, he reached for his cartridges. It was awkward loading a gun while in a tree, but he managed it. Then, holding the musket steady, so as not to lose the prime, he waited.

The British were questioning Matt and Zeb, and Homan could hear the questions. "Where have you come from?" "Why are you here?" "Are you alone?"

Matt maintained a stubborn silence.

"Just out for a walk," Zeb answered.

One of the British soldiers burst out, "I say, shoot them now!"

Another shook his head. "Wait for the Captain."

So there were more coming—one more at least. The odds would be greater than they were now. Homan's finger moved toward the trigger. If he could bring down one, could Matt and Zeb handle the other three? Not likely, without weapons. Instead, probably the British would kill Zeb and Matt and shoot him down like a treed raccoon, to boot.

One of the British stepped closer to Zeb. "Haven't I seen you before?"

Zeb answered coolly, "Have you?"

The redcoat slapped his hand to his thigh. "I have! In Queenstown! Last autumn. You—you're a gunsmith, and you repaired my musket!"

Another one of the soldiers laughed. "That's him! How could we forget that ugly face!"

I was right, all along, Homan told himself. Zeb *is* a Tory spy! Why else would he be in Canada, working for the British? I walked right into his trap and brought Matt along with me!

The soldier who had first recognized Zeb said grimly, "How could I forget the worst gunsmith in the whole of Canada? My musket never fired after you repaired it!" He turned to the other redcoats. "And he ruined the Captain's pistol."

Strange, thought Homan. Matt told me Zeb was a good gunsmith. The officers liked to have him repair their weapons. How could he be an expert gunsmith at Fort Niagara and a poor gunsmith in Canada?

One of the redcoats said suspiciously to Zeb, "You're an American soldier. How did it happen you were repairing English guns?"

"Very simple," answered Zeb. "I wasn't an American soldier then. Can't a man change jobs?"

"He changed more than jobs!" exclaimed one of the other soldiers. "He changed sides. He's a turncoat!"

"Worse than that!" another cried. "He's a spy! A black-hearted American spy!"

Homan was stunned as the truth of the redcoat's statement sank into his mind. Zeb was a spy, but he was not a British spy. If he were on the British side, he would have identified himself to the redcoats at once. Now Homan realized what Colonel Swift had meant when he said Zeb could be trusted. The Colonel was aware that Zeb had done the dangerous and valuable work of a spy for his country. He had repaired guns for the British so he could collect information to pass on to the American commanders. He had ruined the British guns so they could not be used to kill Americans.

And I reported him to Colonel Harris! thought Homan. But he had no time to dwell on his feeling of shame. Now, more than ever before in his life, he must keep his head.

He began to figure a plan of action. One of the redcoats was facing him, but the sun was in his eyes. The other three had their backs to him. If he could just take all of them by surprise. . . .

Carefully he edged out on a limb until it began to bend with his weight. It creaked, and he was afraid the redcoats would hear him, but just at that moment, Zeb asked as calmly as if he were at a tea party, "Where are you stationed? Did you come all the way up here from Fort Niagara to view the falls?"

The sound of his voice covered Homan's movements, and his query occupied the British, who were annoyed at the impudence of a prisoner who dared to question them. Homan reached forward and grasped the branch with his left hand. Holding his right hand over the priming pan of his musket, he let the bough carry him down, down. Every second he feared that the branch would snap with a loud report. To his immense relief, it bent without breaking. Ten feet from the ground he let go and landed on his feet in the snow. At the same time, he shouted, "Drop your weapons! We have you covered!" He followed this by several shouts in deep and high tones, hoping he sounded like a whole patrol.

The British whirled toward the sound of his voice, and just as he had hoped, Matt and Zeb went into action. As he ran forward, he saw Zeb kick the musket from the hands of one soldier and plunge on to plant his fist under the chin of another.

Matt was struggling with the third redcoat, while the fourth leaped toward him with fixed bayonet. Homan lifted his musket. There was a slim chance that enough priming powder was left in the pan to fire the gun. He had no time to add more powder, so he pulled the trigger, and the musket responded with a roar. Homan saw the bayonet that had been menacing Matt fall to the ground. The soldier who had held it grasped his arm where the charge had struck him.

Homan reloaded his musket and kept the redcoats covered while Zeb bandaged the Britisher's wounded arm. Then the three of them briskly marched the prisoners back to meet the rest of the patrol.

On the way, Homan apologized to Zeb. "I saw you hit that soldier outside Fort Niagara and then I saw you take the canoe to Canada—and I thought you were a British spy. I even reported you to Colonel Harris. I'm sorry."

Zeb gave him a lopsided smile. "The Colonel knows all about me, so that's no worry," he said. "I was a spy, an American one, but not any more—and that's your doing, my lad."

"Mine?"

"Aye. The man I knocked to the ground outside the fort that day was a British spy, and thanks to you, he got free and went back to Canada and reported me. I paddled across the river that very night to find him, but I was too late."

"But he was in our uniform!"

Zeb's eyes suddenly had an angry brilliance. "Stolen from a dead American, I have no doubt." He shrugged. "After that the British knew me for a spy, so I gave it up. If they'd caught me in Canada, I'd have been in front of a firing squad before you could say 'Yankee Doodle.' The first part of this month I joined with the regular army."

Homan stammered, "I-I've been such a fool."

"Aye," agreed Zeb. "But you've spirit, and I like that. That's why I chose you to go with me to Manchester this afternoon. I knew you'd be a hearty lad in a fight if we ran into trouble. And you proved me right, or we'd be the ones with a gun at our backs."

"I wish I'd understood sooner that you were an American spy," said Homan. "I wasted a fair amount of time trying to figure you out. For instance, the night before the British came over to Fort Niagara, I saw you stagger out of Hustler's Tavern. I followed you down the road toward the fort till you took to horseback."

"You've the making of a spy, yourself." Zeb chuckled.

"That night I was doing a bit of spying strictly on my own, on our side of the river. The British had their agents over here as thick as plums in a pudding, and I struck up an acquaintance with one of them. I let him think I was a British sympathizer. All evening I drank with that rogue and tried to wheedle some news out of him. I thought he'd never get talkative. He was careful, even in his cups."

"How did *you* keep from getting drunk?" asked Homan.

"Aha! A secret, but I'll share it with you." He winked slyly and pulled his cap forward over one eye. "I had Kate Hustler bring me colored water instead of strong drink. I must've swallowed a gallon of it before the fellow told me in great confidence that the British had a plan to avenge Newark soon, perhaps that very night. He advised me to head away from the Niagara at the greatest possible speed."

Homan listened with breathless interest. If Zeb had known of the attack on Fort Niagara the night before it happened, why had the fort been taken by surprise?

"You didn't run away, did you?" asked Homan.

Zeb said scornfully, "Of course not. I headed for Fort Niagara, but my companion in the tavern must have had an accomplice who followed me, for I was attacked not far from Lewiston and left for dead. The next thing I knew, Lewiston was already in flames. I managed to drag myself into the woods and there an old trapper found me. He took me to his cabin so far off the usual trails, the Mohawks never found it. Soon's I was strong again I went to Hardscrabble and joined up."

"Matt thinks there was treason at the fort," said Homan.

"I doubt it," Zeb answered. "Just carelessness. I could see a difference between our soldiers and the British army when I went back and forth across the river. They have real discipline, they have. You wouldn't catch one of them leaving the gate to the fort unbarred. I tell you, Private Reed, it's too late to start training an army after war's declared. And that's what we tried to do."

The rest of the patrol was waiting with the horses outside Manchester. They had seen a small British scouting party, but had not engaged them.

Afraid of being followed, the patrol prepared for a quick return to Hardscrabble. The prisoners were parceled out to share four of the strongest horses with members of the patrol, and Zeb again took the lead.

Long before they reached camp, darkness slowed their pace. Homan was tired and cold, but he had a feeling that was close to contentment. He had met the enemy and he had not run away. Even Zeb was pleased with him. It was a relief to have the riddle of Zeb solved, even though it was humiliating to have been so wrong about the man.

As he jogged along in the dark, he forgot about Zeb while he mentally traveled the snowy miles to Batavia. What would Molly think of him, he wondered, if she could see him now, going back to camp with prisoners he had helped to capture? Her lively face shone in his mind like a lamp.

Now if only he knew the whereabouts of Guy . . .

It was almost morning when the weary patrol pulled into Hardscrabble Camp. A message was waiting for Zeb Humel to report to Colonel Harris. Homan Reed was also wanted at the Colonel's headquarters.

So tired he scarcely could walk, Homan stumbled down the path to headquarters with Zeb. They were shown into a big room where a dying fire and one feeble lamp provided the only light. A few benches stood about, and against the far wall was a bunk bed.

With a groan Zeb dropped stiffly onto one of the benches. "No doubt I'm here to report on our mission," he mumbled, "but why does the Colonel want to see you?"

Homan went to the fireplace, hoping for a little warmth. "I've been wondering the same thing," he said. He reached for the poker, intending to stir up the fire, but as he did so, someone moved on the bunk bed and sat up. A familiar voice said questioningly, "Homan?"

Homan dropped the poker to the floor. He stood transfixed while a slender young man with tousled brown hair limped quickly across the floor toward him. Suddenly he gave a glad shout—"Guy!"

Chapter 15

ﾊﾊﾊﾊﾊﾊﾊﾊﾊﾊﾊﾊﾊ

Peace

Willows were a misty green and in the woods white trillium blanketed the ground like late snow.

Homan and Guy followed the River Road south toward Lewiston. Shorty, who was with them, ran a zigzag course, chasing the scent of rabbit and chipmunk. It was early evening and a few fishermen were anchored near shore. Across the river in Canada, Homan could see thin spirals of smoke rising from chimneys of farm homes. How different a sight that was from the black clouds of smoke from Newark and Lewiston!

A little more than a year had passed since the cold morning when Homan had found his brother waiting for him at Hardscrabble Camp. Already many people had returned to the land beside the Niagara River to rebuild their homes.

Guy limped along in silence with his gaze on the opposite

shore for such a long time that Homan wondered if he were remembering when he had been a prisoner there. He shouldn't have unhappy memories of that, for he had been a well-treated prisoner. Because of his wound, he had been kept in a nearby hospital instead of being sent to Fort George and later marched to Burlington and on to Montreal as were the other Americans captured at Fort Niagara. As soon as he had been able to walk, he had been exchanged for a Canadian prisoner of war.

Guy finally broke his silence. "Everything looks the same. It's as if the war never happened—except for hard feelings between us and the Canadians. And in time I hope they'll be forgotten."

"Something changed," Homan declared. "The British aren't taking our seamen any more."

"They don't need them now that they're not fighting Napoleon. No, this war was a waste, a complete waste of lives and money."

Guy stumbled on a stone in the road. Homan walked more slowly, but made no comment. His brother was proud, and wanted no notice paid to the limp that was his heritage from the battle at Fort Niagara.

"Bates Cooke said we had to win the respect of other nations," Homan recalled. "So that's one thing we accomplished."

Guy walked several paces before he answered. Then he said slowly, "Maybe. But I think we'll win more respect by years of peace and hard work than we'd ever get by war."

On the road ahead of them, Homan saw Molly approaching.

"Anne's on her way," she told Guy.

"I'll go on to meet her," he answered.

Molly's face had a scrubbed look and she was wearing a blue dress Homan had not seen before.

"Come on," he said. "I want you to see the field we plowed today."

It was a fair-sized plot, for Uncle Oliver had begun to clear the land before the boys had come to live with him.

When Molly had admired the deep furrows that wound between the tree stumps, Homan said, "Guy and Anne will be getting married soon. He has the cabin almost ready."

"Good," said Molly. "Anne might as well move out of our house. She walks around dreaming about Guy all day."

"We own the land together, Guy and I. Uncle Oliver left it to us." Homan looked at Molly and then away. He noticed with satisfaction that he was now two or three inches taller than she, though size no longer seemed as important as it had a year ago. "There's plenty of room in our cabin, but with Guy getting married, I've been thinking I'd build a cabin of my own—say in another year. I'll show you the spot I've picked out."

He led her north along the river bank until they came to a place where the trees formed a half-circle, facing the river.

"Do you think this would be a good place to build?" he asked.

She looked long and carefully at the land, then turned to face the river.

"It's the best place in the world for a cabin," she told him.

"I'm glad you like it," said Homan, smiling at her, "because I don't aim to live here alone forever."